GOLD
&
PLATINUM

GOLD

&

PLATINUM

Top Priority of Your Wad

THE IMPORTANCE OF HARD CASH
LIKE ONE DECILLION OF US
DOLLARS OR A BREATH-TAKING 36
FIGURES PAYDAY

A NOVEL

MICKEL J. CHARLES JR.

Library of Congress Control Number: 2018914941
ISBN: Hardcover   978-1-9845-7356-8
               Softcover   978-1-9845-7355-1
               eBook   978-1-9845-7354-4

Print information available on the last page.

Rev. date:12/19/2018

To order additional copies of this book, contact:
Xlibris
1-888-795-4274
www.Xlibris.com
Orders@Xlibris.com
787869

Capitalism portrayed like a wicked behaviour inducer or a not honorable at all economic system.

MY GOSPEL USA

Once upon a time in America
There was a fellow named George Fox.
And another brother Jonathan Edwards
They preached the Gospel on a horse
across every city in the country.

Oh my USA, Gospel, Gospel, Gospel
Again & again, the Gospel USA
My Gospel USA! My Gospel USA

We traveled all the way from France
Without any resources, we made ourselves resourceful
With hard work and dedication, we made it big
Our successful journey is what we call the American dream

The Almighty God through the Gospel USA
Oh My Gospel USA! My Gospel USA! My Gospel USA!
El Shaddai through the Gospel USA
My Gospel USA! My Gospel USA! My Gospel USA!

Lately, it was the death of Billy Graham
The best preacher ever who has lived on the planet
They said T.D. Jakes would continue Billy's Ministry
The son Franklin is on a mission to reinforce the Gospel belief
We praise The Lord God Almighty for Franklin's successful Ministry

Thanks to The Highest Lord of the host!
God is The Greatest!
Praise the mighty Savior Jesus-Christ!
For saving my Gospel USA
My Gospel USA, My Gospel USA,
My Gospel USA!

EXORDIUM

The gentleman stated that many things happened to him mentally in a way that he wouldn't be able to explain. And, it's the reason why he's ready to describe what's going on in someone's mind when that person seems lost while looking at you. We usually tend to be conversing with probably our inner self stating:

-Tell me what is it that you cannot define factually.

-Listen, it's too complicated of a situation and anyone who has a certain logic would think it's craziness at its best.

-Alright, I understand it looks absurd – just give me a clear illustration.

-Let's take the great NY Dutch Kali (Muay Thai) world champion, Ramon Dekkers, he didn't get to be the best in one night without proper training. Actually, he reached the invisible knowledge of that confrontational art through daily physical study. Then he got the one-shot knockout whether it's a kick or a punch, his opponent isn't interested in getting hit. When anyone gets to such a point in anything, they're able to see things the supposed normal eyes cannot or wouldn't be able to perceive – all of us or the mass, we must trust that person.

-I still didn't get it. What do you want to tell me?

-All that to say, long time ago, some well trained contemplative people saw a Spirit, I mean it doesn't have a substantial form, it can only be in our mind, they call it God, he's pure goodness and righteousness. In Asia, they confirmed that we as human beings can construct such spiritual things or characters – that spiritual presence they've named God hasn't been formed by no one, it exists with no time, no space, without any beginning, nor end.

-You're sure about that?

-That's what the well trained meditative ancients observed, and it's the way to elucidate our origin as human beings.

*

Mainly, the lieutenant thought it was best to never question beliefs or faith, there wouldn't be anything to enable a better understanding. The padre wouldn't hesitate to continue this church service all day long if he had to do it this particular way. He kept reading the Psalms and, precipitously, he said: "Psalms 23, together (referring to the audience):

"The Lord is my shepherd; I shall not want.
He makes me lie down in green pastures;
He leads me beside the still waters.
He restores my soul;
He leads me in the paths of righteousness
For His name's sake.

Yea, though I walk through the valley of the shadow of death,
I will fear no evil;
For You are with me;
Your rod and Your staff, they comfort me.
You prepare a table before me in the presence of my enemies;
You anoint my head with oil;
My cup runs over.
Surely goodness and mercy shall follow me
All the days of my life;

The bewilderment of the assembly was certain as we could hear the last sentence saying:

"And I will dwell in the house of the Lord forever".

The mass was called in memory of Capt Barthelmy "Shepherd" Kemp, fall in combat in Yugoslavia, more precisely in the outskirts of the city of Gospic. The top officer unlawfully put his five thousand men directly between the Bosnians, Yugoslav Army Serbs and the Croatians. The brigade destroyed many tanks and equipment of all sorts on both sides of the three belligerents. It was reported in the annals that the mission was a complete success until he died with two other comrades while crossing an unsafe area of the battlefield. One of the reasons why the U.S. armed forces honored the commanding officer is because the military law doesn't have posthumous condemnation. Capt Kemp could only be a dead hero of the USMC.

They were saying there's no way for them to support mutiny on the theatre of war whether it did provide a victory and a startling one. And, the three stars generals are Americans, notwithstanding the fact beyond the troops many were Canadians, First, Second and Third Vandoos and the Patricias. The inquiry demonstrated the soldiers have heard the rumors of insubordination of their commanders. Finally, the report reached a conclusion it wasn't a lack of leadership which caused that slide of procedure of Capt Kemp, his emotions pushed him to do what he thought was the best action to save as many lives as possible. Nevertheless, those troops were a dream team with the Seals, the Airborne 82nd and most of what is known as Special Forces. The main course of their actions was a systematic sabotage campaign with the purpose of breaking the tools of war of the Bosnians, Yugoslav Army Serbs and the Croatians. The element of surprise was to see the enemy never suspected this efficient brigade would carry such a large scale operation targeting all their war capacities. Welcome to Year I of the peace mission based on the complete dismantlement of the belligerents' war gears of all sorts. We can think and know why the top Canadian and American officers wrote their reports saying "there weren't any professional inaccuracies in the actions of the battle group".

It took more than a month time for Capt Kemp to plan what he thought would justify their tour of duty in Yugoslavia. Since on the field he was the top commander, he saw the opportunity to lead this operation all the way to victory. He carefully recruited more than a hundred Croatians, Bosnians and Yugoslav militaries that were presented to each other as the hands of peace, and both sides agreed to destroy the arms of their respective armies. Both sides swore to don't take a toast before a complete win.

In such a situation, coordination is everything. The plan was to merely create several commando groups that will act in some kind of a blitz. It was clear if both sides wouldn't have the armed forces anymore; it's just fine and better. The order to destroy more than seventy-five percent of all equipment is already given. Everyone knew how essential it was to cut all supply routes and both the Bosnians, Yugoslav Army Serbs and the Croatians won't be able to battle each other. When pronouncing his last speech to the officers of all three forces, Capt Kemp specifically detailed the key to success at war is to get a huge surprise component that the opponent never expected – like when your left flank that was very well protected is about to be taken by the enemy.

When the morning breeze is fluffing the dust on the ground cleaning that same landscape, any soldier on duty feels the twitch to be cured. In modern times, it has ceased to be an insanity to pick such a means of support. Now, three armed groups are motivated to deactivate their own income sector. The satire of being trained to terminate your individual tasks. It could be really sarcastic to do certain things comparable to clashes at war where you may not live to appreciate the compensation. Clearly, we see the prominence of being mighty to guard the social corps, more importantly, its laws that must never be besmirched. The course of action which is about to take place displays the raging hostilities to carry out against law wrongdoers although it's not at all times evident to differentiate righteous from deprived. Those nations of Yugoslavia are all on the evil side by their will to annihilate each other as there's a fabulous wind of peace significantly prepared to overpower them – the so-called: "beat them in their own game."

Many things showed the challenge of neutralizing the means of war on each side of the belligerents equally. Before destabilizing these three warlike army groups, all bulky apparatuses are to be put out of order and the ammo. They can improvise by the use of civilian gears; on a large scale basis, it can't be efficient by being improper. All the requirements of success are there, especially the staffs that know all the places and accesses. Capt Kemp assumed it was time to unleash their actions against these wrongdoers unceasingly, and they will still be active even after the victory.

From the documents that were found, we could read it was a complete three days campaign in which all means of war got speedily annihilated. It was carefully planned according to the disciplined military manner. All the facilities were targeted in a way that an alert would come too late. It was reported in classified documents both confrontational' camps war capacities were completely destroyed at about the same time. The American forces inquiry revealed the plan is to be used in the training of war school cadets. It's exciting to note that when the bases were crashed into by the use of a powerful cement filling in almost every piece of equipment whether it was a truck, tank, plane, ammunitions depot, rifles, the facilities, etc. And, One of the important effect and result was when we saw a base launching an alert or calling to get help, and there was nobody able to provide anything because they were all "attacked" instantly. The good news came in when many soldiers heading the city where they thought they could get some resources, it was a sign of victory.

Meanwhile, there was an active army group of seven to ten thousand men that couldn't be destroyed because they were at war or in movement. The supplies of all kinds were cut off, but it will take several weeks before they can be missing anything like food or ammunition. Again, Capt Kemp open his bag of tricks to show how to peacefully fight an army determined to combat for real not having any idea of peace crossing their minds. It's easy for the officer who knows his job that he was trained to carry such tasks. One of the basics of infantry, according to him, is for the enemy to never know where you are as an individual, a recce group, a battalion or a battle group.

The area of Srebrenica was the most dangerous place in Yugoslavia, and the three enemy groups were at three to six kilometers away from each other. Capt Kemp took the position right in the middle of the three rivals thinking that he will be able to talk to both of them about the necessity to make peace. The soldier messengers came to see the commander stating two bad news: the US supreme command is ordering you to draw back according to the rules of engagement manual, and you'll be court martial for the sabotage actions against the three armies – and, in twelve hours from now, a US Army colonel Lane Perry, will replace you as commander.

With an apparent madness in his face, Capt Kemp told the 2nd lieutenant and the three men including a sergeant:

-Go and tell these generals that I intend to finish all this the right way: peacefully and no one will get hurt. They have my word!

-Capt. Kemp, you're already relieved from your command of this brigade. It's clear; you're not the commander anymore!

-2nd lieutenant Keene, you're under arrest for non-compliance to a superior officer's order to deliver a message to supreme command. Sergeant, take 2nd lieutenant Keene to confinement until we resume this mission!

The entire brigade succeeded in a marching movement at some twenty kilometers on the right side of the Serb's troops to be entirely out of range and forgotten. It was confirmed they were utterly unnoticed as their positions were unknown to the enemy searching for them. It was still not Capt Kemp's plan which is to merely halt this army group. Although there was no danger for them, the Serbs could possibly confront the Croatians and make vulnerable the peace plan so well-orchestrated.

It didn't take a long time before anything considerably changed at war. The two imposters hired by the little secret service of Capt Kemp to replace a Serb and a Croatian general as a superior officer of the Yugoslav Army were already in their position firing intensely on every direction. Those charlatans were able to get in their commanding position with the power to navigate the armies of the Bosnians, Yugoslav Army Serbs and the Croatians where ever they would like to send them. From the standpoint of Capt Kemp, it's not where we carry them that's important, it's to get all their supplies in right hand, far away from them.

Some exact orders were given to expressly tell the army commanders to head straight to their barracks as the supplies were carried very far away from where they could be burned completely. Meanwhile, the little skirmish at the level of the company involving seven sections in total left some deaths, among them, an 82nd Airborne, Capt Stu "Barking dog" Angar, and he put his metal tag with the wrong name through his teeth. It's a way for Capt Kemp to fake his own death because he decided he won't return to the U.S. He carefully handed two envelops for the supreme command to be given to his son, Third Class cadet Brant Kemp, who is studying at the Virginia Military Institute.

*

CHAPTER 1

"Materialistic and capitalist people are the less intelligent individuals of the societies."
-Mickel J. Charles Jr.

Giving away the fact that he doesn't know which means he's going to use, John Barlow always sees himself as the next Canadian tycoon and Prime Minister. The public perceives the professionals as people that always seem prominent than for real. It probably never occurred in our minds that these apparatchiks are holding a very fragile power. Does it happen that some youngsters are dreaming of becoming a protuberant lawyer because of the high responsibility and influences? Again, it is certain that everyone attracts by the thought of having a place among the wealthiest and the most important individuals in the societies. And, what kind of glamour can the fact of living an everyday life close to sickness, murders, disturbing people, controversial issues, violent prisoners and God knows, can bring? The challenge? The salary? Anyway, it is almost surprising when somebody is walking downtown Montreal and see all these firms. Of course, some folks don't think about the way these offices work. Or maybe all the population think they know what is going on.

All the elements concerning the life of a high-level civil officer, indeed never came in the head of John Barlow. Financially, the man did very well, with the meager amount that he was receiving for an operational job at Brunton Wheels, located at the very west part in the industrial park in St-Laurent. For years, John had been robbing banks at gunpoint with an excellent level of success. His criminal activities had started a long time ago before he met his wife, Ann.

John had never thought about laundering his significant amount of cash. He's always saying to himself (in his head): "My cash is where my weapons are."

Even though he's working with what is called "the drop out a bunch," John is a grade eleven graduate from William Hingston High. He can personify extremely well the image of the perfect Canadian student: he's bilingual with a Quebec accent. John takes pleasure sometimes in telling somebody that he doesn't speak English or French. Every year, he can read at least sixty books or an average of fifty. He read all the books of the Quebec French authors, and he's certainly to educated for a "High school guy", like some friends enjoy to call him.

John never got arrested or embarking in a police cruiser. In his solo bank-robber career, he did thirty-seven banks throughout the country. Only in his twenty-second shot, some cops fire at him without hurting any part of his body. When he got home, he prayed to God. He was already married to Ann and he didn't tell her anything about the risks of his dangerous life. John stopped his felonies only three years later, on March the 7th, 1980. On that day, he invented a reason to get drunk with his friends at Le St-Sulpice, on St-Denis Street. Nobody from the people of John Barlows surrounding ever found out about his stealing activities. He looks like the typical guy who he's working for Brunton Wheels - always driving his nine years old GTI or six years old Chrysler Voyager - nothing fancy at all.

On November the 27nd of the same year, John handed out a resignation letter to the management at Brunton Wheels stating that he's leaving his position for a personal reason. Off course, Ann opposed herself to the decision of her husband to quit his job. It's not that John was thinking about all the money he got aside from his robberies or any Retirement Saving Plan (RSP). He was looking at his bank account and the fact that his lifestyle cost him probably a quarter of what he earns and the house on Kildare and Mackle is already paid. John is thirty-eight years old, and he has one hundred and eighty-eight thousand dollars in his SAVINGS ACCOUNT plus twenty thousand in his CHECKING ACCOUNT. Personally, he knew that he's leaving his job because he just didn't want to work anymore at Brunton Wheels or any other place. He just wanted to lead a peaceful life with his wife and their three children, Jessica, Ben and Alice. Since John was born in the fifties, there was probably nothing exciting slightly before his eighteenth birthday or after. He dates many girls for several years like some kind of a philanderer - but he never got accustomed to that style of life - he indeed developed a strong libido by living like that for a while. John is part of the generation who used to listen to ABBA, THE ROLLING STONES, THE CULT, THE TEMPTATIONS, JIMMY HENDRIX, THE POLICE. In a way, it is just to say that John Barlow listens to all the music that he can find - exactly like the high number of books that he reads.

Before the age of twelve years and seven months old, John Barlow had never stolen any money from any institution whatsoever. It's only around the age of nine that he had started to take a few quarters from the little amount which his parents would leave in the house to pay the milk or some other things. But Bill and Margaret Barlow never really mind about the fact that baby-John would take money in the money box without asking them. John's parents thought that he was doing that only to have his own means when comes the time to buy what he wants. And the psychologist said that anything kids like John do at this age, if it doesn't cause any immediate problem, it doesn't matter at all. On the opposite, Father Bentley advised Bill to don't tolerate such a behavior from a kid regardless of the age. And, Aunt Martha supported the advice of Father Bentley. From all the family and professional discussions about John's attitude, Bill decided that their only child was doing very well and there was nothing to worry about.

At the age of twelve, Bill and Margaret wanted their son to live somewhere more in view than their hidden suburb of Truro in

Dartmouth, Nova Scotia. So they thought of uncle Ken who lives on the corner of Kildare and Makle in Montreal, Quebec. After all, Mr. Kenneth Barlow likes his nephew John a lot, and it would be a pleasure to have him by his side like a father and son. And Johns report at Wilfrid Laurier College was one of the best in his grade. He knew a lot about plumbing, renovation and all kind of construction work. A good deal was about to be made because he just bought the house, and John's cousins Isabelle and Yvonne didn't want to take part in any construction work in the house. They cleaned, they cooked, but it was entirely out of the question for them to repair anything. John thought that he could be the brother and the son of the family.

The day of his arrival in Montreal on July the 7th, 1975, John started to implant his saving system when he told the cab-driver whom uncle Ken sent to pick him up, that some other friend was going to drive him. The cab driver gave him the twenty-dollar uncle Ken paid in advance. He walked across town with his luggage along with a city-map of Montreal to guide him to the house located at 4475 Kildare Street. So from the plane, he took at Dartmouth Airport which landed at Dorval, he walked all the way to uncle Ken's house in NDG. He crossed Cote-de-Liesse road passing by Rodolphe-Page - an airport street. Then got all the way to the Town of Dorval and shuffle East on Lakeshore to Ville Lassalle thru St-Joseph Blvd in Lachine. In John Barlow's mind, everything is always easy no matter what, even if you don't know how to do it.

From his thirteen years of age to fifteen he exerted himself as a paper-boy for La Presse and he didn't spend even a penny of his pays. He delivered the article from August the 25th 1975 to September the 30th 1977. For the two years and one month, he gathered the total amount of thirteen hundred and thirty-seven dollars. John Barlow started to work at McDonald's one week before he stopped delivering the La Presse. He applied the same policy at McDonald's Restaurants: not even a penny was spent.

John keeps having the same thoughts like memories. The first one is in 1968 while he was at his parents' bungalow in Dartmouth, Nova Scotia. He remembered sitting in the living room around Noon. In his mind, he was proud of his eleven years old of age. The fifth symphony of Beethoven was playing, John's bewildered eyes would stay wide open for some seconds, at the most, on the decorations of the house - the posters of Martin Luther King Jr. along with some paintings of the twelve disciples and some family pictures. The living room was so inspiring with all those memorable things.

Papa Wemba, the African musician and his world beat rhythms mixed with the images that are flowing on the T.V. put John in a mood where he was freaking out. Actually, there was a preview for a documentary where we could see Hitler, Mussolini, De Gaulle, Churchill, JFK, King at the march on Washington with his famous "I have a dream!". Then, another preview showed Onassis, Hughes, along with some other wealthy people of the time. Behind his closed eyes, like a massive screen on the wall, there was a real life-size image of himself - an adult futuristic portrait. On the side, there are pictures of some actual moguls, Ted Rogers, Bill Gates, Presidents and chiefs of States. This day-nightmare of John didn't last very long.

In that same living room, John's face wasn't recognizable. For him, his eyes became heavy, and he had to concentrate like putting emphasis on them as they were closed. When they suddenly open for another short period of time, it was the music, those same African sounds of Papa Wemba and Kofi Olomidé. Now, the entire place is turning like when he's playing in the schoolyard by turning himself around a pole. He didn't have to move because everything moved round and round by themselves. As he pulled back, he was focusing on each detail like a movie camera.

Being thoroughly awaked now with all his conscience, he looked at the kitchen before leaning on the side of his bedroom's door. The time hadn't changed - he thought - it was still noon. John stood up and walked to the kitchen. He was close to the kitchen cabinet jar as he brought his forearm and hand while he opened the jar. The money, change mostly, which were quarters, dimes, nickels, pennies and some little bills of one, two and five. John took a one dollar bill, two quarters and two dimes and he walked all the way to his room and put the money in the little pocket of his school bag.

The time of the day had changed for sunset, and he finds himself in the front door alley. He walks back to the living room and halfway from there, there is the sound of keys in the main door of the house. His parents entered the house and John was face to face with them. The same African music of Kofi Olomide, Papa Wemba or Madilu that was playing on low, just progressed at a higher volume -in his mind like a dream. While his parents were speaking to him, he couldn't hear anything most of the time because different classical and African pieces of music were playing - louder when somebody was talking to him. John's mother just embraced him as his father touched his head. And John suddenly said:

-"Mummy! Mummy! Mrs. Holms told me again that my grammar is excellent!"

-"Yes my baby, my dear lovely John, you did it again," his mother mentioned.

-"Everything indicates that my son is a genius. Excellent John! Keep up the good work," the congratulations of his father.

-"Yes, dad!"

-"I just saw the guys with their hockey stick. Why don't you join them?"

-"That's exactly what I was thinking, dad."

John took his hockey stick from his room wardrobe and walked out toward the back door of the house. His Converse tissue sneakers were at the door. He put them on and walked back to the kitchen and smooched his mother.

-"John, Baby! Don't go too far!"

-"No Mummy! It's in the school backyard!"

For years, he kept the bad habit of playing hockey on the streets closed to his house while cars were dangerously passing by. John was dicking and snapping a ball with his hockey stick as he was walking to go play. And he was saying at a mid sound power: "Richard again! Richard again! Richard again! And score!" Maurice Richard would have certainly appreciated being his teammate or opponent. A kid is undoubtedly never too young to confront the elders. When wars break out, they enemy never ask any question unless there is a ceasefire.

He still lived on a phenomenological level where he remembered the delightful moment of his childhood mostly. John saw himself in his memories as bright as a far away planet under the lens of an all-powerful telescope, arriving at the schoolyard and most of the players were there. The entire game with all the actions and his excellent performance is still there lurking in his mind. He did score many goals. The talented eleven years old hockey player will make it someday.

John got back home for supper, thinking for sure that some other family members will be there to applause him. At a certain distance, he remembered seeing that back door where he liked to pass by after any game. Before John opened the door to come in, he felt that somebody was there hiding to surprise him, and he wanted to show that he didn't know. For him, it couldn't be nobody else than aunt Martha, his second mother as he's been always considering.

Purposely this time, he came face to face with the woman. He was right, the person was Martha.

They're still in the Back door's alley. Aunt Martha was looking at him closely in the eyes as she spoke laughingly. She touched his right arm and felt his growing pectoral:

-"Oh! Johnny Baby! You seem to be very happy and in great shape."

-"Aunt Martha! I'm always waiting for you to come here."

-"You wanted to see me, I'm there! What do you have for me?"

John started to laugh ruefully as he crossed his forearms. Then we saw Aunt Martha taking John's left hand and walked him to the dining room - his mother already put everything on the table. His father was coming from the living room as he got there. It was a feast pretty much like the castle's one - exquisite and sophisticated. Everybody took a sit as John stayed close to his aunt. His father did the prayer. He remembered clearly each of the food bowls as the four persons were serving themselves. Everybody started to eat at the same time as a regimental mess dinner. Before anybody started talking, John was imitating Natking Cole:

-"Unforgettable, in every way..."

-"Keep on singing Johnny... I love that!", aunt Martha said with excitement.

-"John is an anthropologist just like his dad. We can already see the first sign of the world's best scientist. And the last marks you got are there to prove it," the positive remarks of Bill Barlow.

-"My little will be a happy young man beyond anything else. You hear me John, I want you to enjoy your life", Margaret Barlow replied worryingly.

-"As an anthropologist, he will go to England and all over Europe along with Africa where he will learn all his roots." His father laughed and said: "Johnny, You're a Massa!"

-"Bill, what are you saying? Being from Africa doesn't mean that he's necessarily a Massa", the objection of Margaret Barlow.

-"Johnny is a Massa just like he's a Scottish knight that carries great battles with bravery," the immediate retaliation of Bill Barlow.

In John's mind, everything started to mix up like a long video clip with everybody eating and talking. Then suddenly, he was all freaked out again with rapid snapshots of all what happened down there: the house, school, friends' houses, parties, Halloweens, homework, hockey games with friends, trips to the arenas, basketball games with friends and many more.

John was now thirteen years old and ready to leave Dartmouth, Nova Scotia. He didn't forget anything. John and his parents had already agreed that he will leave Dartmouth to go live with his uncle in Montreal. Mrs. Barlow showed a lot of emotion compare to his father who was very calm. John's eyes were wide open as he was thinking with his mind very far from this parental discussion. And suddenly, he smiled and told his mother:

-"I'll come back often anyway. It's not expensive to come here from Montreal."

-"Yes, you will. I'm sure about that," Margaret Barlow told him.

-"Anyway, It's normal for the kid to leave the house and go make his future." His father looks at him in the eyes and says: "You're a good boy, John. I think you should know that we raise you to be independent and responsible. It's maybe our choice to make you leave Dartmouth, but you can always refuse."

-"No. I'll go to Montreal. Uncle Ken is just like you, dad."

His father left the dining room to go watch T.V. in the living room. It was on another channel. He puts it on CBC. We are on April the 4th. They're announcing the assassination of Martin Luther King Jr. So John and his mother are rushing to the living room to see the news. On that day, he remembered the emotions and the grieves on the faces.

-"They killed that good man, mummy. Why? Because he's not suppose to be a good man," John said to his mother.

-"No Johnny, Baby. Don't say that."

-"I want to know why they killed him - with a rifle. Anyway, he probably died from a pistol like the one that agent Dunlow, the policeman, is carrying."

-"John, Rev. King is a good man. He's what we call a militant. All militants are in constant danger... of getting a kill, half of the time. Rev. King is surrounded by enemies, of his own group sometimes. What most likely happened is that beyond all the white racist who is against him, somebody from the official government probably issued an order to have him down - to kill him if you want. The way he died tells us that a professional soldier killed him. Now, I'm not a political scientist, neither a journalist, but I do know that people like FBI director Hoover and some other people of his rank don't like Rev. king at all - they're probably the ones that gave the order to kill Mr. King."

-"So Dad, I heard a girl in my class whose father is a lawyer says that any government is base on the principle that "the king can do no wrong," which would mean that it's a good thing that Rev. King got killed."

-"I wouldn't say that."

-"What would you say, then."

-"Obviously, the government did plot to kill the Reverend. I would say that they did the wrong thing."

-"What should they have done instead of killing him?"

-"They should have agreed to his legitimate demands which are mostly base on the end of segregation, once and for all."

-"How can we know if the government could have agreed to Rev. King's demands and didn't want to? Or if they wanted to settle but they couldn't."

-"They probably didn't have the right persons to team up with Reverend King and do the necessary changes.

-"Yeah... Yeah... It's still unfortunate to kill a good person like the Reverend."

John had a sorrow face as he seemed to be thinking deeply without finding an answer. Their living room was sad - Bill, Margaret, and John were sitting close to each other on the long colonial sofa. Three months after, they were in front of the house around noon, when John, followed by his mother and father carried his luggage to the family car. Since it was July the 1st, some people were moving in and out of the nearby houses.

-"You didn't forget anything? Your baseball glove, your basketball ball...," Bill Barlow said to John.

-"Nope. I have all my stuff."

-"What about your uncle's gift?" Margaret Barlow asked him.

-"I have it with me."

-"I guess... it's time to leave now," Bill Barlow said.

His father's car left the front of the House by making a U-turn to actually head the autoroute to Halifax Airport. John kept looking back at the house and the neighborhood like he had some kind of nostalqia. The place where he grew up and spent an entire childhood.

In his memories, there is no day more sacred than when he left the Canadian Maritimes. The autoroute leading to the Halifax Airport is dazzling, in the sense that there is hardly enough cars to cause a circulation problem. You can take your automobile and be sure to drive toward the destination at a fast pace. And his parents make the rides in the car so enjoyable with their jokes and family stories. They are always talking about all kinds of things concerning John. It's mostly noise which could be heard from their conversation because they are talking too loud.

-"Mummy, Yvonne is still in grade ten. She has a lot of difficulties," John told them with a concerned face.

-"Isabelle is perfect. Her marks are almost like yours. She told Kenny that she wants to be a lawyer," his mother replied in a positive mood.

-"Did she told uncle Ken why she wants to be a lawyer? I guess she wants the money."

-"Nope. She simply tells him that she likes argumentation... and the law make us know how big we are as a person."

-"I don't quite get it... all I know is that the girl that I know who's father is a lawyer said that he goes to Toronto often... and he makes a lot of money."

-"Is that what you want for yourself?" Bill asked him.

-"Maybe. I don't know. It's good to make a lot of money..."

-"You're right my son. A respectable high salary is a good goal for you."

-"I guess it doesn't hurt at all to do a job that you like and gets paid very well."

They are taking the exit for the airport. For some reason, the parking lot is very crowded. Although they can't go in very fast, they hustle their way in, and they got to the entrance door. Inside the airport, we hear the usual flight arrivals and leaving times. Of course, the voices of the crowd of people can be irritating sometimes. We see pilots discussing while they're walking - along with the stewardesses. They knew already that the flight for Montreal is leaving in an hour and a half. The three are walking while eating peanuts and talking about all kinds of family things - the cousins, uncle Ken's job, the house, cooking, and other things.

-"So, you think you'll like Montreal. It's a vast city," Bill commented.

-"Everything will be fine. Isabelle always wanted me to come down..."

-"You'll miss us, sweetie... I want you to call us often."

It was time to go. Before passing through the flight door, John hugs both of his parents at the same time and embraces them. Then he passes through, the doors and takes the plane. It is packed inside. He eats the food that they're serving and sleeps during the entire flight. The plane landed on time. Again, this airport is crowded also. It's a weekday and a lot of activities are going on. Nobody could come to welcome John. Mr. Kenneth Barlow, his wife, and their two daughters Isabelle and Yvonne are on vacation in the Caribbean.

There is a taxi driver whom John's uncle sent to pick him up and drives him to the house on the corner of Kildare and Mackle. The taxi driver had a placard saying: "WELCOME TO MONTREAL MR. JOHN BARLOW!"

-"My uncle sent you..."

-"Yes! I have to drive you to the house," the cab driver responded.

-"It won't be necessary. I have a friend of mine who is already here to drive me."

-"That's fine. You want the money... I mean..."

The taxi driver is giving to John the money that Mr. Kenneth Barlow paid in advance. It is some kind of a habit of John to always spend as less as possible or nothing at all. A city-map of Montreal which was in his luggage is now between his fingers. John thinks that no matter how far it is, he will walk all the way to the house.

While on his way to the house, he meets a girl.

-"Do you know how to go to Hampstead? I mean Cote-St-Luc, Outremont...," John asked her.

-"It's far from here. I'm walking home, you can follow me and then you'll go your own way to Hampstead."

The walk on the Airport roads and the streets of Lachine was fun and made him feels that he will like the city. John and the young girl named Ann McIntosh chatted for quite a long time. She walked with him all the way to Hampstead and exchanged their phone numbers. He appreciated her kindness, and she's also a beautiful girl. Indeed, they're thinking about seeing each other more often.

He did come to Mr. Kenneth Barlow's house many times - but it was different nowbecause he lives there. It's a beautiful evening. John already knows how the house looks like. He takes the keys from the side of the house and opens the back door where he gets in. The entire family hides in the house to make a big surprise to John. As he enters the living room, everybody just splashes him with creampie and say: "Welcome to Montreal, Johnny!" The entire family just surrounded him like he was a brother and a son.

That evening, everybody was in the dining room talking to John almost all at the same time. John was eating while the others were snacking with chips, peanuts, and vegetables.

-"So, how is Margaret? Bill told me that you're a genius with some very high marks."

-"Mummy is fine. She's always talking about you..."

-"What does she say about me... she's about to quit on Bill..."

-"She says that you're a nice person... You're an important part of the family. Things like... you like me a lot."

-"You goddamn right... I like you a lot. I said it several times, Bill and Margaret made a son for me... And now they completed everything by sending my son to me..."

John is not quite finishing to eat that Isabelle takes his arm pretending to show him his bedroom. In fact, she wants to chat with him far from all indiscrete eyes. Isabelle is not shy at all to think about having those kinds of boys date with John. These kinds of ideas never actually cross John's mind. And it's not because of his uncle - who would have indeed agreed even if they're cousins.

Isabelle's head is on John's legs who is sitting on the bed. John is shy to be too intimately close to his cousin. He's even afraid to tell her. The principle to don't be intimate with family members is right for

John. In a way, Isabelle should forget about her erotic ideas about John. He finds all kinds of excuses to avoid close encounters with her. always The girl purposely spends a lot of time in John's room. He keeps kicking her out continuously. With the time, John develops the talent to rebuke her funnily. Isabelle seems to be very patient and never abandon her goal to conquer the heart of her cousin.

Nobody has ever proved for sure that the initiation of a suburban and almost a country boy like John to the big city's style of life can be dangerous and maybe deadly. John was about to find out.

It's been two weeks since John's arrival in Montreal. Apart from Ann McIntosh whom he can't see often, John doesn't have a lot of friends. At some forty kilometers from Montreal, a very young American gangster named Raymond Washington is about to pass thru the border to come to meet some crime partners. The very rich bandit is traveling with his lawyer and his driver along with a bodyguard. He's twelve years old. Although he's never been accused or prove guilty of anything, he's well known in the media for having gang relations. When passing thru the border, he had an argument with the guard.

-"You're Raymond Washington?...The gangster."

-"There is my passport... like you can see, I'm Raymond Washington. I'm not quite sure about the last kind of nickname you just say..."

-"You mean you don't have a criminal file. How is that? And you're a minor. Sorry man..."

As a strange coincidence, Raymond Washington's crime partners are supposed to meet him in the park where John is playing baseball. Raymond is very good at what he's doing because he has close to four years experience. Actually, he has two kilos of cocaine in his clothes - he has to collect the money and leave. The baseball game is over, and John was introduced to the guys who were playing with him. Some of the guys know Raymond very well. As Raymond approaches his partners for the deal, he asks:

-"Who are these motherfuckers?"

-"Some chump huppies playing baseball. Nothing important."

-"Who's the one on the right with light skin face... I've never seen him."

-"Hey! You! The chump down there. Come here!"

The guys close to John tells him that he is the one who is being called. Since Raymond is leading the area, even if he's very young, nobody ever question what he says.

-"Man... John, I think Raymond is calling you."

-"Who is Raymond?"

-"You don't need to know. Just never mess with him... He can kill whenever he wants."

John is not scared or impressed at all by the power of Raymond Washington. Actually, John answers to Raymond's men by saying:

-"Why don't you come here?...Whatever your name is.""Niggar, You want me to come to you? You still have a mind... or something... Bring your damn ass here!" Raymond Washington yelled.

-"No. You are going to bring your damn ass here....You don't know me!"

Raymond Washington strolls toward John. He told him that he's new in the area and he should take it easy. John told him:

-"Whoever you may be, I certainly don't need your advice. Keep them for yourself."

-"I'm going to tell you this once, you stupid ashole. My guys can cock one or many damn pills in your thick head. So, now just beat it and I'll pretend that I didn't hear anything from what you said. Get the fuck-out of my face!"

John is close to Raymond Washington while he is talking. As the argument progresses, they get closer to each other. He merely pushes his opponent and says:

-"Fuck you man! I already told you that I don't need any advice from you."

They wrestled for at least five minutes. John got Raymond with two hooks at the head. Although Washington is solid, technically, John wins him.

None of the guys who were with John approached him to do anything. Washington's guys came and help him stand up even if he wasn't hurt at all. Then Washington states: "Fuck'n stupid nigger can't even do any algebra, physics or chemistry and he wants to fight. Do you have money at least, to buy our stuff?"

-"I can sell you some, and you can make five hundred percent profit."

-"I'm not going to repeat myself. You don't understand that I don't need anything from you."

Raymond Washington turns his face and leaves. Before he leaves, he tells his guys:

-"I don't know where this damn nigger comes from, but he's stupid. It doesn't matter anyway, he's not black enough for me. Don't kill him, hey! If any of you shoots on this motherfucker, the bullet is useless."

After that dangerous encounter on that particular day which was a Saturday, John went to his house, and he didn't really think about what happened. Some friends told Isabelle about the fight in the park, but she didn't say anything to John. Mr. Kenneth Barlow was informed too, but he's not the type of guy who's going to treat John like a child by starting to ask a lot of questions.

On Monday, it's John's first day of school at William Hingston High in Park Extension. The regular morning activities of an entire family who is preparing themselves to leave for work and school take place in Montreal for John, for the first time. Isabelle prepares his lunch and hers. John already has his paperboy job for. And Isabelle tells John:

-"Ann called for you yesterday while you went to the grocery. She wants you to call her back."

-"Yeah. I'll call her back."

After school, around sunset, he's at the Footlocker sports store on Jean-Talon Street. He shows his natural bargainer talent with the salesman and gets out wearing a nice pair of sneakers.

-"How much is that Nike, there?" he asked.

-"I can have you twenty-five percent off the normal price."

-"Okay. I'll take them!"

The first game of tennis with Ann wearing his new pair of sneakers got him to think that life is fantastic in this city and in general. He's telling her about his Midget-AAA hokey for next year. She keeps staring at him while smiling. John is showing his happiness to be with her. Admittedly, she is already impressed by the hero's sporting accomplishment as she feels grasping him intimately so firm that any other female should forget their chances.

For some reason, he feels that summer rolls in fast in Montreal that year. And it is time for something else perfect to happen. He comes back to see his parents with Mr. Kenneth Barlow, Isabelle, and Yvonne. It is a time of the holiday. The entire family spent five days in Dartmouth. The big family reunion was delightful. Everybody kept on joking almost every day on each other in the most friendly way possible. At some point, we would tend to think that the house was too small for them all. Even aunt Martha was there for two days with them.

His sixteenth birthday caught him on the action as he came back to Montreal. He starts to work at McDonald's as he's been seeing Ann for quite a while and nothing serious was happening. Finally, Ann feels like it is time for them to have a close intimate relationship. She invites John over in the absence of her brother and her parents. John is on time, and the bell rings.

-"Who is it? John... are you there?"

-"Yes, it's me. Open the door. Are you scared..."

-"Okay. Just wait for a second..."

John gets in and sits down in a very unusual way. Ann can't keep her burning desire to kiss him for the first time. Strangely, John is not aware of anything, and he's not looking forward to whatsoever. Ann's parents have the kind of long half square sofa. The house is nice with all its decorations. Ann is busy in her room - when she finishes, she walks to the living room and seats close to John. Then she says:

-"What do you want to listen to? I know your passion for music. So don't be shy. Tell me because I have almost all the records. Choose one and I'll play it for you."

-"I want to listen to Natking Cole, Marvin Gaye, and Charlie Parker. You sure, you have them?"

-"You're lucky, I have all those songs."

The music is playing, and John couldn't stop imitating the songs. Ann tells him that he's annoying. She reduces the volume and tells him:

-"I don't know how you feel about me, But me I'm very attracted to you. Actually, since the day we first met I'm always thinking about you and me in a relationship."

-"I guess now we're old enough to love each other and commit to each other. What do you think?"

-"Yep. This would be just fine. And all my family already know about you. I told them everything in the smallest details."

-"What did you tell them exactly?"

-"I told them that you will be my husband someday."

Ann approaches herself more close to John and kisses him on the lips. She's not fully aware that John is used to a lot of girls and he wants to have more than a simple kiss. She refuses him politely to go under her skirts. So he explores her nipples and kisses her neck and rubs her body. Ann has a lot of fear because she doesn't want to lose him over some refusal of sexual relation. She is thinking that it's only her way of doing things and nothing else.

-"For now, I just want us to kiss each other. I just feel that it's not good for both of us to get involved in more things than that... I mean..."

-"Why is that... You're scared or something... I mean to get pregnant... or your parents, maybe..."

-"No. Not at all. I simply feel that I love you a lot and that if we start taking down our underwear would kind of messing up everything. You understand that?"

-"No. I just think that you're scared of something. There is nothing more natural then to sleep with someone we love."

-"Do you love me? Are you ready to commit to me?"

-"The love question looks complicated. I can commit to you, of course. Let's keep hanging around like before and then will see. If we like it...We..."

-"We... what? You want me to sleep with you and let you go. Am I some kind of hole that was made to give you fun?"

-"Ann, I don't know what's going on with you, but you're over-reacting. Relax okay, if you don't want to do anything, it's fine with me. Now stop you bullshit feminist thing there... Hey!..."

Ann didn't say anything more. She gently caresses his ribs and gets her hand to his neck. Then gazes lovingly at him before kissing him again. She gives him a beautiful breast and abandons herself entirely in his arms. In any movie, it would have been very thoughtful and creative to pull out the camera slowly before closing by a global view of the entire living room with the two lovers who are in each other's arms.

In John's mind, the years flow in Montreal like fast winds. And a good day came - just one month after his seventeenth birthday, he graduated from William Hingston High in Park Extension. Of course, it wasn't the school where a parent would most likely send his kids, but John did his best and finishes at the highest level in all the disciplines. Granting the fact he's a good football player, an excellent boxer, and can probably perform well in all the other sports like hockey, tennis, basketball, baseball, John Barlow had his career plan according to his parents' advice. It's not that Bill and Margaret Barlow didn't want their son to achieve some kind of a very high academic level or becoming a sports star, they didn't want him to spend too much energy for nothing. They also felt that Dartmouth was a little bit too crowded to provide a future for their son even the smallest ever. So the day before he comes to Montreal, his parents told him these words that he will never forget: "find a job and try to perform as you try to don't spend too much of what you earn."

On that birthday time of October 1977, John Barlow began to search for a job. He got hired by a customs broker in the Old Montreal to work in the mailroom for thirty-six hours and a half per week at an hourly rate of three dollars and ninety-five cents. John got promoted six months later to the position of rater at the same salary. After four years, he got tired of working in a brokerage office with all the paperwork. It's not only that, he found another position at a pharmaceutical company where the salary conditions are a lot better. Again, like in all the other jobs, John Barlow hardly spends his money. And now the house is his because uncle Ken bought another one in TMR on the corner of Brittany and Foster for $495 233.00 taxes included. There is only $8 800.00 left on the mortgage for Kildare and Mackle - John paid it to cash in one payment.

CHAPTER 2

John Barlow had a great life at Benson Pharmaceuticals with a fix gross annual income of $38 365. He got married to Ann McIntosh after his first year on the job. The company got him into the research training program to provide technical assistance. Everything went very well, and he reached the position at $42 876, per year. In his, thirteen to twenty visits every year to Bill and Margaret in Dartmouth, Nova Scotia, the happiness on his face was very obvious. It wouldn't certainly be false to say that, what was going on at the job helped John to build some kind of an everlasting relationship with Ann. For some kind of a hat trick, he did three banks in that same month for the significant amount of $546 thousand by using a new stealing technic. The little boy from Truro, Nova Scotia indeed ignored the deep psycho-sociological reasons that pushed him into the robbery business.

Nonetheless, we all know that life has its alternations, and everybody is subdued to that rule - which means that any situation can change at any time from its previous state or any other state. Even if financially, John has many things that he can rely on, stealing cash is an everyday business that he owns. Some people will probably say that he can open a shop, create a company or make some investments instead of full-loading fire-arms to go rob. It's very logic to say that this kid is sick in the head. He has enough money. And, his uncle is well-off.

On the morning of November the 5th 1986, an internal memo announced that Benson pharmaceuticals will be restructuring its activities all over the country and most likely some jobs will be lost.

John was already told that his position won't exist anymore and his training program can help him get another job in the industry. Some other choices would have probably led John Barlow to some other things. But for now, he's a gunman. And this is entirely different from somebody who would be just stealing, not shooting and killing people on his way when he's carrying out business. So he doesn't believe a word in the idea that he will undoubtedly find the same kind of job in the pharmaceutical industry. And, as a matter-of-fact, he won't find a job because these people told him so.

The situation was frustrating because he knew for sure that these people who are managing the company mind their own pocket and don't care about him. John felt that he had to do something about that. On the morning of January the 3rd, 1987, John Barlow fired several bursts of bullets at Vice-President Tom O'Neil in an extraordinary professional manner. As a criminal, John Barlow never does anything in some kind standard way. The day he killed Tom O'Neil was a Saturday - and he didn't expect to "waste" him that day. Why someone would decide to randomly go to his office on a Saturday? How is it that John got him like he was waiting for him? There is only one answer: John Barlow was seconding Brant "Pepper" Kemp for twelve years in his mortal activities involving bikers, mobsters, yakuza and all the craziest and dangerous of the planet that has their embassies in Canada - Montreal, Quebec.

Brant "Pepper" Kemp was badly wounded of four to five projectiles from a big caliber weapon. He had to kill a man and take possession of his suitcase containing $1.5 million. Something went wrong, and he got involve in a gun battle with the man's three heavily armed bodyguards. "Pepper" eliminated all the guards and the man, took possession of the suitcase with all the cash and drove his car to a safe place, at thirty kilometers away. On that day of June, John Barlow was sixteen and was coming back from anight shift at McDonald's, it was eleven o'clock. John saw "Pepper" before he was aware that somebody is looking at him. What did attract the curiosity of John in the man is because the canon of his HECKLER AND KOSH submachine gun could be seen at twenty meters away. We are on Van-Horn avenue in Hampstead. John told "Pepper" that he knows and understand the complexity of the situation but he's not a police officer, he only wishes to help him to cure his wounds. There was nobody in the house because everybody left for vacation. Pepper was lucky because he had already lost a lot of blood. The man is not an amateur. He sends John to get some special dressing and some tonic water. John Barlow still ignores that it's not every day that you meet a guy like Brant "Pepper" Kemp. Undoubtedly, the best gun-man on the planet.

It's not entirely sure that people are introduced to crime because of their social class. John's case is altogether different. He read a lot about some great men who were murdered, like Martin Luther King Jr., JFK, and others. Somewhere in his mind, he's thinking that killing for cash or else must not be that bad. Why these great people didn't defend themselves by shooting back? The killer was undoubtedly at the power position at this particular time. John's felonies can be linked to a day of June while he was walking on St-Laurent Boulevard. On that day, he saw a man coming out of a National Bank branch with a backpack and an automatic pistol in his hand. The man was running very fast when a car stops and picks him up. John stayed there, and eighteen minutes later, the police arrived, and a crowd gathers in front of the bank to watch. Five minutes after that, John walked away from the scene of the crime. When he got home that day, he attended the news, and as expected, there was a report on the robbery. Like it wasn't enough, he searched for it again in the Newspaper. The article said:

"HOLD-UP FOR $150 thousand. The St-Laurent Boulevard was very crowded yesterday as many gathered in front of a National Bank branch to watch the police after a quite experienced bank-robber stole some $150 000.00 at gunpoint. The robber pushed the cashier against the wall as he entered inside the offices and threated the manager with his weapon by saying: "you better open that goddamn safe and give all the money or I'll kill you. You got it! I'll blow up your damn head!" The manager, Mr. Gene Ligeti emptied up the cash register and put everything in the robber's bag. Since the manager couldn't open the safe, he gave some extra bills that were nearby. According to the witnesses, the robber was in such a hurry that he left right away after his bag was full of cash. The customers who were inside the bank think that the amount was more than $150 thousand."

After being more than sufficiently informed about the robbery, John shook his head slowly front to back, telling himself that bank-robberies might be very good to provide him a lot of money. He talked to himself thru the bathroom mirror, pointing his finger like a pistol and saying: "I will treat them and get the cash." John walked to his room and took the card from his office - the card that Pepper gave him two years ago. He called the number.

-"Hello! Mr. Kemp please."

-"Myself. Who is speaking?"

-"John, you remember me?"

-"Yeah. Yeah. I remember you, of course. Call me 'Pepper' man."

-"Yeah, Pepper, how you doing man? I need a little something..."

-"What do you need John? Don't be shy, you can speak out man."

-"I need some weapon."

-"Yeah. Okay, there is no problem. I can get you all the weapons that you would need. Listen, why don't you meet me at 5611 Tyler Street in Lassalle....Make sure you got some balls man..."

-"Yep. I'll be there right away."

Pepper wasn't thinking that he's meeting John for something serious. It's a routine for him to go see someone and give him a couple of guns. There is no problem if he would be framed. He has some kind of permit to do any crime. Why do some criminals are scared of getting caught? Pepper never even thinks about such a thing. He did ten months in a military jail for an accusation which doesn't even exist in the army's law books. He's sure that the world is strange and a strong man never hears any problem. And so many things are mixed up just to get people out of their minds. They talk about God, rules, and sins although they're doing everything - the most forbidden. For him, John is something entirely different from what he used to see - he hopes and bets that he's right. It doesn't matter at all that a 'home' kid wants weapons. Souvenirs from military school are coming out of memory: "If all enemy men are dead, you can tell yourself that you've done a great job!" Pepper was thinking that he's not allowed to kill any other thing than the enemy. He remembered that he was a little bit lost or partially asleep when the instructing officer passed by him and said: "Wake the fuck up! You damn lost! Did you hear what I just said?..." Pepper had a way to concentrate that helped him to survive such a strong education. He was like a wild animal trained to bite and destroy. In his world, there is no rule. He doesn't do something because he feels like doing something else - unless he was ordered to carry another action.

For a mysterious reason, Pepper seems to know anything that looks good invisibly. His car is parked on 89th Avenue. He's sitting in the car, and from his mirror, he can see John coming. John is about to pass by the vehicle when he calls him.

-"Hey man! How you doing?"

-"Fine. Where you've been?...Make a long time..."

-"Nothing special. Just business as usual. Lots, lots, lots of cash... So, come on in if you want a get what you need. We're going to drive a little bit to my place..."

John was thinking that taking chances is always very important. Here is what looks like a kind stranger who has a lot to do with guns and hardcore crimes and he's with him. It's comfortable to know that Pepper has no intention of killing him. John is not afraid at all. The first advice of Pepper to him about having courage because of what he asks. He starts to understand that he's leaving that crowd of people who obey to enter the small group who leads and orders by the power of the barrel. It's bizarre that such a big event happens humbly. John will obviously learn that anybody who shoots, controls, indicates and most of all, leads.

There is no reason for him to call the fortress his place. He doesn't go that often to what looks like an armory. Pepper spends his time to his houses. And, he never stays too long at a place in particular. Now, the outside of the fortress doesn't give the impression that it is like a military armory. It's similar to a typical farm depot. In fact, it's a solid construction made of two feet thick concrete. The measurements are something like a rectangular two hundred meters by threehundred meters. It goes to the two-floor underground.

Usually, there is nobody in the compound. When Pepper reaches the entrance door to enter his code, the machine indicates the presence of people inside. He already knows who is there. Then the door opens, and they come inside the fortress. John and Pepper are walking through the alleys of the compound. Although John didn't see it, there are weapons installed everywhere. They enter the most significant room in the fortress where we could see almost five thousand firearms of all brand. Suddenly, Pepper stands in front of John and tells him:

-"I don't want to be too nosy, but I would need or prefer to at least an idea of why you need some weapons?..."

-"I just want to make a lot of cash. Yeah... just cash..."

-"Are you aware that you can make absolutely all that you want, the way you want to do it? Why this weapon thing?"

-"Before I answer your question, I would like you to answer it yourself."

-"Me, I use weapons because that's what I know. In other words, it's my job. I ask you that question because I don't see any reason in that goddamn world why somebody would want to enter a profession like mine."

-"For the exact reason that you entered in yourself."

-"Listen, man, I don't want to be a pain in the ass. I'll be short and sharp: I'm a Marines, and it's far from me to advise anybody to choose that position. You can have plenty of money without any weapon or..."

-"Let's carry on Pepper. I just want you to give me some guns... and that's it. Maybe we'll be in business together... God knows..."

-"Yeah. Now you're talking business. That's good news."

-"You said that we can do all that we want. Is it true? So, why so many people are not doing what they want?"

-"I have no idea. All I know is that it's the truth..."

John Barlow and "Pepper" became good friends. Pepper initiated him to all the death tools that exist - most of all, the logistic support staff. They often go to the country house in the Laurentians where Pepper has his most important weapon hide-out. The kid is fascinated by weapons - the brands and model like McMillan, M-16, BROWNING, COLT, BROCK, AK-47, FAMAS, S-80,SMITH & WESSON and many more, including some anti-aircraft and anti-tank devices. After a couple of years hanging out with Pepper, John Barlow became a commando soldier without a uniform or a military affiliation.

They kept going up north to shoot with weapons. It is mostly on weekends - they use at least twenty to fifty kinds of weapons: pistols, machine-guns, shotguns, and riffles. Pepper and John are often talking openly about crimes. First, Pepper congratulates John for the series of robberies that he carried for the past weeks. He wants to introduce John to more hardcore crimes like contracts to kill, drug exchange and extortions. But John tells him that killing deals would be attractive. As they walk in the compound, the subject of their conversation is about past criminal actions and the everyday life of a criminal. The jokes and the loud laughs make a funny friendship for them.

After a while, Pepper starts to talk about a challenging contract for John if he wants it. Pepper tells John:

-"There is a prominent American businessman for half a million dollars. He's supposed to be in Canada tomorrow before noon. The only information we have is that he's coming by the Vermont border to go to Ottawa and we have his pictures."

-"Humm... You want to give it to me?"

-"Yes. But think man, there is no plan or strategy, you go by yourself and do the job like a total stranger. I don't know you, you don't know me, nobody knows anybody."

-"Alright. What about you?"

-"You don't want to know the shit I put myself in. Just do what you have to do. Now, remember, you should never come here alone without talking to me before."

-"Fine. I'll do everything clean and sparkless."

Some three hours after sunrise, John was already at the Vermont Canada-U.S.A. border. He's lucky because there are not a lot of people crossing thru. There is a pair of goggles in his hand that he's not currently using. Most of the long town cars are well verified, especially when there is more than one person on board. John is riding a Suzuki GSX motorcycle he plans to quickly leave as soon as he sees the businessman's car. He has a car at fifty kilometers from the border with a military version M-16 with grenade launcher, one Uzi and two 9-mm pistols. The plan is to shoot the target in the car while riding the motorcycle and explode everything with several shots of a grenade.

The suspicious car is coming, and the man matches perfectly the picture which he has in his bag. Now, John is leaving the border in front of the vehicle at a long distance. He's riding very fast to ultimately lead them to have time to take his weapon and gets ready to complete his mission.

John gets to his car which is safely parked in a rest area. He's grabbing the M-16, cocking the two pistols and putting them inside his vest. Then, he's looking for the Lincoln that he's carrying the target. The car is seen from afar. He recognizes the vehicle and the businessman, and he let them pass by as he waits two minutes. Then John starts to chase the car with his weapon well concealed and ready to shoot. John is on the side of the vehicle as he unleashes the bullets on the two passengers and the driver to finally shoot three shots of a grenade to completely burn the car. Then, lets the weapon go as for the automobile that he abandons to complete the mission intelligently. John rides the motorcycle far enough, brings it in the bush to burn it with his vest and helmet. For an excellent victorious day, he already spots a cab stand that he uses to come back to Montreal.

In the criminal world, its known among scientist that crime is an activity or a constant conflictual situation that has far more adrenaline than war and some other things. John's game has since travelled more than a thousand miles in Europe at Mr. Christophe Fanengen's office in Switzerland before sunrise, the next day. The target that Pepper took several years ago before he met John happens to be one of Mr. Fanengen's close associate. Since Mr. Christophe Fanengen is Europe's top crime boss, and he's informed that Pepper killed his friend, he wants to kill Pepper at all cost and all his people are already looking for the top gunman. Fanengen is well known in the crime community for his governmental relations and the large size of his gang.

Pepper receives several phone calls from a lot of people who inform him that he's a target. At least seven of the callers emphasize the fact that his life is in great danger which means he should take the necessary precautions. One of the guys tells Pepper that his case is hopeless. He did three phone calls to some independent and former gang member criminals to bring as many people as possible to help him. Pepper says these words to his contacts:

-"I want to see people like "CRAZYBULLET," "COLT," "BARKING-DOG", "GAGE," "RAGE," "WOLFMAN" and all the crazy ones that you know. Make sure you bring everybody to the Laurentians fortress."

In the morning, at Fanengen's home in Geneva. Two men are coming to see Mr. Fanengen to advise him to take stronger measures against

Pepper. The simple contract to kill Pepper is not enough. One of the men tells Fanengen:

-"You know that this man has a fortress. We can have the authorities to raid his place. Our people in Canada can do that for us."

-"Yes. I will call Interpol to take care of him. He killed Salvan Badin for $1.5 million. Why! Why!..."

-"Very unfortunate indeed... I always say that our business is the most useless. We are menacing and forcing people to get what we want..."

-"Salvan was my friend, my best friend. We must punish this Pepper, like they call him..."

Mr. Fanengen shows a lot of emotion on his face. Then, the two men leave with their suitcases while Fanengen is about to take the phone to call his contacts at Interpol.

The police are already out of Pepper's case. Now, the Canadian national security office headquarters of the S.C.R.S. takes the file. Some high-level officers from the Canadian intelligence services just read a significant police report about Pepper's criminal activities. It's stated in the writings that the police organizations all over the world are worried about "the military equipment that Brant Kemp has, his numerous gang's contacts and the fortress in the Laurentians." The officers enter the director's office to discuss what to do about the report. First, the director asks:

-"Who is he exactly? That Brant Kemp... I have been told that he has his army just like the government..."

-"He is an ex-Marines officer, quite good soldier... actually a commando. He's American with Canadian citizenship. He spends some months in a military jail... and for several years now, he's been doing all kind of criminal activities for millions of dollars... murders, drug trafficking, extortion, you name them..."

-"What do you guys suggest? We should raid that compound..., " the director questioned.

-"Why not... At the moment we're speaking, Brant Kemp is in the compound with a lot of his people... and they're not about to leave... Sir, I suggest that we take extraordinary measures against that man. We should have Air force, Army, in a joint effort to completely dismantle everything...," the officer replied.

-"I agree. Arrange yourself with the assistant-director and give the assault," the director ordered.

The assistant-director calls the Canadian Forces headquarters and asks for Colonel Remy "Hyena" Thunder to lead a task force to destroy a criminal fortress. The colonel is told to kill everybody in the compound.

Although John carried out a lot of dangerous actions with Pepper, he remained some kind of a silent partner. And Pepper never told him a lot of other things for some security reason. Was Pepper working for some kind of a hidden official institution? Not at all. It's only that as time goes by, the man was getting into more trouble, and he didn't want John to have anything to do with that. Pepper is already informed that some influential people are quite interested in having him down. He's assured that there's nothing he could do to stop that from happening.

Pepper started to gather his people around him. In a week and a half, the counter-attack group is formed: fifty-eight of the most notorious killers that the world had ever produced form an all-around defense to help Pepper. Most of the people that he called are there. Among the group, we find "RAGE," "COLT," "WOLFMAN," "BARKING DOG," "GAGE," "CRAZYBULLET"- they all have an impressive file concerning the number of people they killed and the extremely high level ofviolence that they use to do so. Each of these guys is very rich.

John Barlow is very far from all this. Pepper didn't invite him to that very violent feast. For any member of the world criminal industry, this is some kind of a dream occasion. It is a time to develop and to satisfy a monstrous appetite for the challenge at the bloodiest possible level. Can Pepper count on all these guys loyalty to keep him safe from getting killed? No. "Barking-Dog" and "Crazybullet" have the contract to "waste." Pepper - they are opportunistic, and they won't hesitate on any occasion.

Actually, they already placed TNT all over the compound with remote-control detonation in case something goes wrong.

Pepper started to worry after a while because he knows that the guys who want him dead will never send that many people. He began to think that the strategy would be to plan an "inside job." Who beyond these fifty-eight guys would be ready to play against him? He doesn't have the answer to such a question. After all, what puts him in great danger is that he's not a former boss in the criminal community. So he doesn't lead any group that belongs to him. Even if he can gather a lot of people like he did, there still no concrete ties to keep the group together. It's very easy for turncoat like "Crazybullet" and "Barking-dog" to sneak in. Now, Pepper's mind is overheated like it was boiling. He can't stay in place. Pepper is trying his best to push away the idea for John to be part of the action. He called "Colt" and some others to see what they think:

-"Do you guys think I can fall on the rounds of an insider?"

-"We never know man!" Colt told him, shaking his head left to right.

-"A contract is a contract. There's one on you, and God knows who has it. Just keep lock and ready to waste the idiot!"

-"The sucker is right here eating with us!"

It looks like Pepper got the challenge of his life. He can't even pull back anywhere. There is no way out. The man who is after him is Kristof Fanengen, the business partner of the man he killedthe day he met John Barlow. Mr. Fanengen's crime connection have at least three hundred years of existence. For these people, there is no difference between the words "legal" and "illegal," they're both the same. Which means that Mr. Fanengen controls drug sales, prostitution rings, arms sales, and many more - for some billions and billions of dollars. And today, he wants Brant "Pepper" Kemp dead and nothing else.

-"I can tell you one thing, Pepper since I know for long - I know the person who wants you dead," Colt told him.

-"Who is that damn coward?" Pepper asked. "So I could get him myself where ever he's hiding."

-"Lion" Fanengen," Colt said with fear in his eyes.

Now, Pepper is mad, and it doesn't look like he can have a clear idea about what to do to disentangle the situation. If he succeeds in killing Fanengen, they'll get him back sooner or later. The solution would be to bargain Fanengen's life. In this case, there is an apparent problem: Fanengen is not the type of person who is going to negotiate in this kind of situation. So, he is going to kill Fanengen and try to have better protection around him.

Fanengen probably doesn't think that there is a way for Pepper to eliminate him. Actually, if Fanengen knew that Pepper reunited sixty-two enforcers to protect himself, Pepper would have been dead right now. The only information that Fanengen has about Brant "Pepper" Kemp is that he's the best gunman on the planet and not an organization leader. The worst thing Pepper can do is to try to negotiate with his deadly follower. Pepper better hurry up because news can travel at light-speed sometimes.

Pepper is in his bunker-office with a GLOCK and a TOKAREV full loaded at his waist - the South-African STRIKER is cocked, ready to shoot. In that little fifteen meters square place, there is probably more than $500 000 000.00 in cash - small and big bills. That room can also be transformed into a DCA tower. After so many years, the man put up an impressive defense station. Obviously, Fanengen must spend a lot to get Pepper down to his grave.

-"Mr. Fanengen, a stranger for you," a bodyguard said calmly.

-"Hello! What's going on?" Fanengen said with his heart pounding very fast. "He's what?"

-"Pepper, he knows youwant him trash," the informant said firmly.

-"So what do you want me to do?", Fanengen asked.

-"Call for more fire-power and the job will be done." The informant assured him.

-"Do you think it's time for our official connection to come in?" Fanengen said worriedly.

Of course, it's time for Fanengen to use his official connection in a case like this one. We are deep underground into a place where probably nobody from the public has ever been. There is certainly nowhere so well hide than the real criminal underworld. Everything is already considered a threat to national security. And that's precisely what Fanengen had in mind.

-"Gentlemen, we have orders to destroy that compound with anybody inside or at less than five meters close. No arrest, just deadly rude force." Colonel Remy "Hyena" Thunders said to its army task force that belongs to the SECRET SERVICE.

Now, Pepper's compound is located at Fifteen St-Jeanvier Rd in Mirabel, fifty kilometers away from Montreal's Downtown. Colonel "Hyena" Thunders is happy. He will be able to operate just like a standard search warrant to an illegal criminal fortress.

They have four times the forces of Pepper with more equipment, of course. I mean missiles, artillery, seven helicopters as significant assault support. The plan is to do everything quick and clean. The boss of the entire operation which is the assistant of the secret service's Director, precisely told Thunders that he doesn't want anybody and especially the journalists to know the extent of the force that is being used. Thunders understands very well what the Assistant-director means because he already did an operation which was about the same: they had to merely locate some biker members and head-shot them - no arrest, no freeze.

The operation is called PREDATOR, and its goal is to destroy anything that is at less than five meters from the compound called

-"NEST." Each group depending on the equipment that they use will have a PREDATOR number.

-"PREDATOR 1-1, calling PREDATOR, message over," the commander of the three airplanes squadron said.

-"PREDATOR 1-1, this is PREDATOR, send a message, over," the base answered.

-"PREDATOR, this is PREDATOR 1-1, NEST is visible - 1-AGM-PHOENIX ready to be dropped on the NEST," the pilot sent the message.

-"PREDATOR 1-1, this PREDATOR, just drop 1-AGM-PHOENIX on NEST, over," the base confirmed the mission.

-"PREDATOR, this is PREDATOR 1-1, 1-AGM-PHOENIX is on its way to NEST," the pilot shot the missile.

From that moment on, the artillery and the helicopters give the last blast as the commando on the ground move in to "clean up." The GPMG's (General Purpose Machine-Gun) surrounding the compound is just basically making sure that there are holes everywhere. And then a special section trying to pick up all the pieces to erase all traces of the weapons that were used. Some two hundred soldiers are clearing the whole place and resuming the mission by killing the rest of Pepper's guys. But some of the guys along with Pepper pull out in some kind of a checkpoint and return fire successfully. Most of them died.

Conceding the fact they were gravely defeated, Pepper escaped with two other individuals. Since it is impossible to have a good count of the dead bodies, they don't know if Pepper is alive.

Now Pepper called on to John Barlow to enter the game. We know that since John was laid off from Benson Pharmaceuticals, and then he went to work for Brunton Wheels. And now he left Brunton Wheels because he resigned and want to live a quiet and peaceful life. But just like WORLD-WAR II caught all these seventeen years old guys, John is pulled by Pepper's situation to enter a more dangerous zone of criminality: the making or the beginning of a gang.

John is having breakfast with Isabelle and Yvonne while Mr. Kenneth

Barlow is reviewing an office speech. Then a television news report by a well-known journalist specialized in criminal affairs saying:

"At around 7:00 p.m. yesterday, the police raided a biker fortress violently in the Laurentians. Many weapons were found in the compound along with four gang members that were present at the time. The fortress was completely destroyed afterward to prevent it from being inhabited by other gangs. An authorities' spokesperson explained that the compound's destruction was planned a long time ago when the police information department was aware that the fortress was serving as an arms depot for several criminal organizations. We still don't know the extent of the forces that were used, but when we look at what is left in the rubbles, it's just to say that it was very lethal."

John is shocked by the report because he thinks that Pepper is probably dead. If Pepper is alive, he will surely call him very soon. He doesn't really care about being late for work. Actually, everybody just left for their normal daily activities. John is still hoping for Pepper's phone call. After fifteen minutes, he decided to go for work. When he gets to the front door, his cell phone rings:

-"Hello! Pepper, it's you?"

-"Yes, it's me. Man, I didn't want you to be there. We kill some of their guys too. Shit, it was nasty with…"

-"What happens? I know the news on T.V. is false."

-"Of course, it's not true. Man, there was a big firefight yesterday. They raided us with airplanes and they shoot all kind of shit…"

-"Why? The fortress has been there for a long time, and they knew…"

-"…because of some other problems that I had… Listen, John, things will become bigger now, I want you to meet me at 5645 Georges Street in Laval. We have serious business to talk about."

-"Alright man... I'll be there this afternoon. Let's say 14:00."

When John gets there, he finds Pepper in a completely different mood. It doesn't look like he wants to start chatting with anybody. Actually, he seems so stern that John has the impression that he wouldn't beable to talk to him about anything. After all, it's Pepper that called the meeting. He certainly has something to say. John is very silent just like the two other guys, "Blaster" and "Eveready." Then Pepper calls John in the room that is temporarily changed into an office. He's telling John about the creation of a gang called "WESTSIDE-CONS." Pepper explains to John the idea to have him in the legal or not criminalized world like a deputy, minister or just as a lawyer. Pepper tells John that only money would stop his plan.

-"I formed a gang called WESTSIDE-CONS. It is my wish to hand a membership card - you can refuse if you want to."

-"I want to be a member," John said with no doubt in his face.

-"Since you're Mr. Perfect - never got caught - thirty-seven banks-robberies and some other stuffs. I would prefer to have you in the legal system with all those apparatchiks, deputies, ministers, solicitors - I mean the one who holds power. You know if we control the one who holds the power we'll have the power," Pepper told him with a calm voice.

-"I don't mind at all. The idea looks good. But I can't imagine for now how all that is going to happen. You must know since it's your idea. For myself, you know that there are not a lot of things that I ignore... but...," John said with a doubted face this time.

-"You know John, I was trained by a man I will never forget, he died in Panama - MARINES Capt Timothy "Spetznaz" Verneslov. When joking with me he always said: "2nd Lt Pepper has the gun, but he doesn't have a goddamn penny. Get the fuck out of my face, you're no good for nowhere!" The Cpt was referring to the fact that I was beyond the rare officers that don't sale the Army gears on the black market. And the last words of the Capt were: "you're just pissing me off. I'll tell you something, your damn PM has been bought, my Governors, your deputies, everybody... the whole nine yards... what do you think Mr. Canadian... you think everybody did their SAT, their Bar exam, their 'LEAD-7' to be a General, no Pepper... nobody did nothing... everybody just pays... just hand out a BIG-AMOUNT-OF-CASH... Then he would point out his lips and say: 'Oh! Brant "Pepper" Kemp wants to be a professional officer... what a nice goal... but inappropriate for our world down this earth..."

-"What does all this means. Can you be more specific?" John said with a worried look.

-"I don't want you to be like me, John. Start thinking about the real world and stop being a criminal just for fun. I'm going to put you in the official system with BULLETS and specifically HARD CASH. A lot of people has been reunited, and we will act in two weeks from now. Be ready Mr. Deputy John Barlow."

Even before the weeks planned by Pepper, several high-level civil officers of different provinces are being not only threatened but gun down by the WESTSIDE-CONS. Most of the law enforcement institutions are infiltrated. Pepper makes John realizes that if it ever happens that the application of the LAW is not based on the FORCE of the ones that are applying it, they'll be out of business. He sends a messenger to the Quebec Public Security Minister and the General Solicitor to ask them if they wish to have an armed confrontation in the streets of Montreal and the suburbs. Yes, they've been very accountable to say no and negotiate to keep the peace everywhere.

Also, the criminals have shown that there will be a peaceful society only if they have what they want.

On the first week, Pepper gets in contact with two high-ranked officers from the Canadian Armed Forces who are working in Ottawa.

Then he and John went to dinners with some ambassadors and several prominent CEO in the country. Pepper also talked to some imposing business families of Canada and the US. John and Pepper always say that they're managingtheir own company and they are looking for partners.

After about a month, they have created some significant connections all over the country. Nobody ever thinks that they are part of the criminal world. A lot of friends were supporting them in all their companies. Of course, the streets of Montreal became very dangerous with frequent gunfights and execution by the WESTSIDE-CONS. Actually, Pepper's gang had some kind of a development plan, and they were systematically conquering the drug sale territories by killing every opponent. Leaders from the three police corps are partners of the WESTSIDE-CONS. Pepper has a lot of friends in the police because he is a peaceful guy that always informed them about some key actions.

Pepper's file is blank now - courtesy of his cop leaders' friends and some excellent political connections. They're even thinking about leading Canada one day because they are beyond the one that has the power. The investments that belong to the gang are so impressive that Pepper's decisions have the power to fluctuate the markets. Since John already knows everything from the economy to probably nuclear physics, Pepper had to study for a while. And they're both prepared now to occupy some very high-level position close to the wealthiest and the most powerful of our society.

Even though everything has been going very well on the economic front, the massacres of the gang can always backfire at Pepper. It's only Pepper and some key members of WESTSIDE-CONS that were identified by some other enemy groups like Fanengen's connection. The risk of being shot is always pending on Pepper's head - not John Barlow.

During the years, John has been very successful in his criminal activities. Now, with Pepper's gang, the "WESTSIDE-CONS," the future looks promising. He has more than a lot of money in cash, at least $25 million. John is the millionaire with an easy life walking downtown Montreal for shopping maybe - not really; just taking a drink like walking to clear his head. He's getting out of the restaurant and comes face to face with Ann. She kisses him on the cheek and says:

-"Hi, John."

-"How you doing? We can say that makes a quiet..."

-"Yes, six years... very long time... Where you up to now?"

-"I'm working, and I have my business... nothing extraordinary."

-"Do you mind if we go back inside? I want to talk to you..."

-"Not at all. And... Where you up to yourself?"

-"I just finished university, and I'm working for a magazine....in other words, I'm a journalist."

John and Ann are now sitting in the restaurant. Ann has a dessert and a juice. They're talking just like when they used to know each other some years ago.

-"This looks good... I guess you read a lot."

-"Of course, you know the game... Name me a book you think I didn't read."

-"Lady Chatterley's Lover, D.H. Lawrence!"

-"Nope. Never heard of."

-"Measure for Measure, Shakespeare!"

-"Nope. But I know Romeo and Juliet."

-"Come on... Everybody knows this one..."

-"Hum... John, I want to talk to you about what happened at my parent's house several years ago. To be honest with you, I still think I was right. And... You know, during all these years I never went out with anyone."

-"Why, it could have been fun... for you. I mean you didn't find any guy that pleases you. There are plenty..."

-"You sure you're not hiding something? You seem to be hiding your emotions, your feelings."

-"Why would I hide something like... All I can tell you is that if a the girl is pretty... she's pretty, and that's it!"

-"So, you think I'm pretty. That's all..."

-"Yeah. And I assume that you are smart enough to know exactly what you want in life."

-"Yes. That's correct. And you know what? I want you."

She approaches closer to him and kisses his lips. They hug each other to become girlfriend and boyfriend again. As they leave the restaurant, a slow dance song starts to play like it was a way to welcome their new reunion. John walks with Ann to her apartment. She's insisting on John to come in. He can't because he has some other crime business waiting for him. When kissing John, Ann felt something hard by his hips; she didn't know that it was a loaded handgun. They keep on hugging and kissing several times, and John promises her to come back very soon.

Now, he's so skilled in felonies that somebody would tend to think he learned it by studying in a book. The most surprising is that nothing looks abnormal to him in what he's doing. He's a professional who is doing a job. John takes the cab until he gets to Ville t-Laurent close to a bridge that separates the suburban municipalities. From there, he embarks in a car that was there for the purpose. He's at twelve kilometers from the place where he has to kill three gang members for the WESTSIDE-CONS to take possession of a very lucrative drug sale territory.

He arrives at the place which looks like a gas station with a little store. The three targets are there with some other friends. Somebody down there indicates the three objectives to John. He takes the car to the air pump, and the three guys are close. John gets out of the car and pulls out his two automatic pistols and literally empty his clips on the men. Then, he quickly takes the steering wheels to leave the area as fast as possible. When he gets to the bridge, he merely abandons the car on the street and crosses the bridge by foot. Then, a stolen vehicle was there waiting for him. He drives the car straight to Ann's apartment.

For the people who are looking at him, it appears noticeable that he's living on the edge with a constant death possibility pending on him. John never sees anything threatening him. He doesn't think whether the job is exciting or not. The person in charge of the task is himself - and nothing else matters. One and only one thing makes what he's doing easier for him to the numerous contradictions of human's life in general on the planet. Although somebody finds or simply obeys to rules, reasons, principles, it's still morally challenging to determine a certain logic. A reasonable person does good and a wrong person evil actions. Anybody who is in front of John's gun is indeed punishable.

The underworld has ranks and according to the structure, Pepper and Fanengen are on top of everybody - because they're targets? Nobody is looking for John at the moment. It doesn't matter at all if they would be looking forward to killing him. In his mind, everybody is falling when he passes by whether he wants you dead or not. Is it faith? Another one of these ancient ways to let other people die and for him to live? He knows nothing about that. Just a way to inquire how some people get to make miracles like he does. Pepper is far from living that way. There is blood circulating in his body like most people. In fact, the contract is on him in a similar way to a life-threatening disease. Why he doesn't use John's tricks? It's like anything else: everybody shoot as they're being shot at but not all of them die. There is no secret in pressing a trigger, aiming or bore-sight before taking a position to eliminate somebody. John wouldn't know the proper advice for a person to live like him.

CHAPTER 3

On January the 28th 1990, while on business travel in downtown Toronto, Pepper escaped luckily to an attempted slaying. A sniper fired three shots on his car on Dundas Street, killing one of his bodyguards named "EVEREADY," a highly skilled Sergeant. He had a military funeral because he was still on the reserve list of the Army. Of course, Pepper's press services cover up everything so well that nobody suspected his illicit activities.

As time goes by, Pepper's profile as a very skilled businessman is growing, and some people are thinking about him to become the next CEO in the telecommunications industry. On his part, John Barlow is progressing faster than predicted in the government command structures. He talked a few times with the Prime Minister, and he has a few good friends in the Liberal Party in Quebec, Ontario, and Nova Scotia. John doesn't have to worry about his eventual rise to the highest Legislature of Canada. But, John Barlow is in some kind of an entirely different situation than Pepper - because he is now thinking about an economic system with optimal production and distribution. Will there be a currency in such approach? What would be the commercial relations between the countries with such a system? John was being asked to teach economics at some very prominent Canadian universities.

Since the day he met Ann in downtown Montreal, it became a habit to spend hours and hours at her place. Actually, he goes there so often that it's now his house. He always rings and then enters. When he gets to the door, she breasts him joyfully. They go straight in the bedroom, and they pull each other's clothes off. We couldn't distinguish anymore who was over who. The two naked bodies mix so well as they roll left to right and vice versa. They form a young couple with insatiable sexual hunger. They sleep for, and they wake up around midnight. John starts to talk first:

-"So, you were thinking about me all these years... I'm sorry, I try to be too practical when a lot of real things can be purely theoretical. You're probably right... I think I love you..."

-"You think... you're not sure then... John Barlow, are you trying to patronize me because we slept together and you've enjoyed that? Man! You don't think that it's time for you to grow up and stop your dick thing there..."

-"Calm down Ann... Take it easy before you do anything that you will regret for the rest of your life..."

-"Are you threatening me?... Get out of my apartment!..."

In any couple, furies are habit-forming. It happens once, and it keeps going on over and over. John puts on his clothes very fast and leaves the apartment. He is very calm. Of course, from the look on his face, we can tell that for him Ann's disputation wasn't serious. He gets out of Ann's building and walks for two minutes. The phone is ringing, it's Pepper.

-"Hello!"

-"Everything is going alright man?... You seem to be very happy..."

-"Yeah. Laval was a piece of cake. You'll probably hear it in the news tomorrow."

-"No. I didn't even think one moment you would have any problem to do that... Man, I'm calling you to invite you to come with me to go to New York tomorrow. I have to see my beloved Mary. You will see, she's got so many beautiful friends..."

-"It's okay. Are you taking the plane? You have a criminal file... Don't you...?"

-"Don't worry you about things like that. You should think about making a lot of powerful friends for our business to grow... In a short period, we'll be legalizing the money as soon as we make it and these people will help us....Man, I got a tell you, I will get married very soon."

John heads to Pepper's almost hidden house in the West-Island the same night. They talk on the patio and then Mary calls Pepper to confirm his trip to the U.S.A. John is talking to him about Ann.

-"Man, I guess I don't have the trick with women... My girl was so mad yesterday; she even gets the guts to kick me out of her place. Now, I really don't know what to do with her."

-"You got to take care of business like a man... Just call her right now."

-"It's 3:00 a.m. She'll be more..."

-"Just do what I'm telling you. Call her right now, right here..."

-"Okay," the phone just rings.

-"Hello, Ann!"

-"John! It's you? Do you know what time it is?"

-"Yes, I know what time it is. Are you still mad at me... for nothing?

-"Listen, I thought that after all these years, you would become more sensitive. I love you, but you seem to be so cold and rude. I can tell you that what you say doesn't go with your face. What are you hiding?"

-"You mean I would have another girlfriend that I'm hiding from you..."

-"Maybe! Or something else... God knows what..."

-"Let me reassure you that none of this is true. Six years have passed since I didn't see you... Be a little bit more cooperative and help me find my way with you..."

-"I have to go to sleep now. We'll talk tomorrow."

-"Yeah. That sounds good. Hey! Do you want a come to New York tomorrow with my business partner?"

-"Okay. Call me at around 10:00."

Apparently, John remembered passing by the Dorval Airport in some entirely different situation. And, being with Pepper is a clear sign that life is not a cake yet for him. He still has to send many other people to their graves. Since Pepper has a criminal record, he has another passport that belongs to somebody else. John introduces Ann to Pepper who shows himself very polite and obedient to women. They manage their way in the crowded airport to finally get in the plane.

-"You like to go to New York? I mean, do you find the States interesting..."

-"I often go on the West Coast because of my job."

-"Ann is a journalist for a magazine."

-"What kind of subjects do you cover mostly?"

-"Arts, fashion, music... kind of things like that... What about you... I mean, what kind of business are you doing?"

-"We have two plants where we make plastic products for our customers all over the world. Now, we're looking forward to an expansion where we'll create two new plants in the U.S. along with some other diversify transactions... The future looks good if we accomplish that plan. Some six hundred percent profit, like two to three hundred million dollars for John and me."

-"Ann, do you know or ever heard of Mary? A world renown model."

-"Yeah. Mary Simpson. I talked to her at least three to four times. She's a very nice person."

-"She's my girlfriend, and we're about to be engaged. I just love her; she's so sweet. I just can't wait to marry her."

-"I never saw you with her. Actually, I never ask her about her love life or more precisely, her boyfriend."

-"Yes. It's me, her lover forever. The only problem is that I'm a busy man; it's a problem that I watch closely. Anyway, she knows how much I love her even if I can't always be with her."

Ann is very close to John, playing with his hair as she gives him a strange look before she resumes the conversation with Pepper.

-"I'm not sure if I can say the same thing about some other people..."

-"What do you mean? I'm sure that John loves you a lot although he might not always know what to tell you exactly. A real man is a man that always knows precisely what to say to his wife... every day. The day a man is too sure of himself with his wife can surely be his divorce day. Before I was a businessman, I was a Marines elite officer, andthat teaches me that I can never be careful enough."

Ann laughs a little bit and keeps rubbing John's neck.

-"John, you should listen carefully before I leave you for someone else."

-"No, you're not... I would never accept that. Nobody will replace me alive..."

It's John first time coming to the Long Island Airport. They arrived in the Afternoon. He's been always thinking that Americans are so independent economically from the rest of the world. From his point of view, they can stop all importations and America would live like a king. The friends from New York are not criminalized. They're mostly professionals.

A limousine takes them to the mansion outside Manhattan. Ann is amazed in front of that kind of luxury that she was never part of or related to. The front and the yard of the mansion are fantastic. There are a lot of people in and around the mansion. Pepper is constantly introducing his friends to John and Ann. Most of the people are prominent specialists in their fields. Indeed, some of them are senators, Governors, high profile lawyers from L.A., NY, Philadelphia, Atlanta, Miami and else.

-"I'll pass the Bar here and in Canada. What do you think?"

-"It's your career. Of course, I would encourage you to become great in whatever you choose."

Pepper introduces John to the Governor of Pennsylvania. The Governor tells John that he's already registered as a lawyer in the State of New York. Also, he states to John that the Ambassador will call in Montreal in the next days to have him register there too.

It's not all the time that a particular activity is fun. There is nothing more accurate in the US and especially in the streets of NY. Is it a divine verse that to get to a specific peak of power and wealth, it is an obligation to pass by NY and its restaurants? Late in the Evening, the four just get out of the limousine, and they're walking toward the entrance of a Caribbean restaurant. Even before they get in, Mary couldn't stop talking to John. In all, the two couples give the impression that they knew each other for a very long time.

-"So, you're Pepper's close associate. Since all those years, how come, I never saw you?"

-"I guess it's probably because everything is going very well... We should never be seen unless we're successful. You look exactly like the Mary that Pepper talked to me about... beautiful, charming..."

-"Mary, were you in Milan for the big show two weeks ago?"

-"Yes, I was there. It was fabulous. All the girls fall in love with the collectionof Martino Navas."

-"John, we know each other for at least seven years now... Right?"

-"Yeah. Six years and more."

John stands up and tells them that he's going to the bathroom. Mary finds a way to keep on talking to Ann. Pepper is not talking to anybody for the moment. Finally, they get off the table thinking that John is about to come back from the bathroom. Looking toward the toilet, they see John who is coming. They walk out the door. When they get on the sidewalk and wait for the limousine which is slow to come. They're all looking outside as the limo leaves the city streets to go on the freeway. Everybody is speaking at the same time. Nobody seems to really mind about understanding exactly what is being said. They're all cackling and enjoying themselves.

The night rolls so fast. And, when the morning came, it's like everybody woke up at the same time. After preparing themselves, they're having breakfast together. Then Pepper and John started to walk around as they come close to two businessmen from the South Coast who have several offices in Canada.

-"I can guarantee you forty percent increase every quarter for the next two years... depending on the market performances, you can get more, of course."

-"Now, we need some papers... like civilian titles that can give us to certain positions... I mean licences..."

-"Very easy, don't worry you... Our two countries are financially linked together... What would be your next cash investment again..."

-"More than two hundred million dollars... Same time, the same place..."

-"That's very good... don't worry for even a second. We'll make sure that nobody ever refuses you anything in Canada and the U.S.A."

-"Do you often go to Canada?"

-"Yes, I mean of course... My company has many offices in Canada..."

At a certain point, it's logic to think that nobody knows who owns that mansion. Some so many people meet here to strengthen their business relations. Now, they're all leaving to go take the plane on Long Island.

Mary is coming to Canada with Pepper.

-"Pepper, I want to talk to you about something. I mean... about a business."

-"What is it darling?"

-"I want to have a chain of clothing stores."

"There shouldn't be any problem for that. Get some people and put your idea together and I'll make the check for the amount of your choice. To tell you the truth, I'm sure it will work."

In their minds, it's probably the last time they take public air transportation. Again, as some people get rich, they have different feelings. They're already thinking about other situations where there would be fewer people - in other words, no crowd. It's time to get on the plane. John is holding Ann's hand. Pepper is talking to Mary. Now, they're on the plane looking for their places. They sit down as the plane starts its taxi before lifting off the ground. The big United Airlines airplane that is carrying them is gaining altitude just like their little group is getting higher in the society's command structures. It feels good to be in the skies close to the ozone level. With the difference that their group is protected by entering the world's business establishment. Some people are well known and wealthy, but they've never been part of anything so exciting and all-powerful. They make a point of the newscasts with their bankruptcies and assassinations. Indeed, the advice of the Gettys, Hughes, Kludge, would be to tell them to don't think about justice and rights, but to obey groups and force. Most, if not all head of states survive because they secretly agreed to the powerful interest groups' decisions and wills. The other ones get shot at point blank and close range. It's like the events that happen on the planet keep following the same rule as exact social science.

Two hours later, the plane lands at Dorval Airport in Montreal. Pepper is going to his house with Mary. John follows Ann to her place. When they were in the flight, Pepper gave John two crime jobs to do in the next days. One of them is in Toronto. The turbulent Canadian-American city never indeed hosts assassinations of people in the style of John. Obviously, it's a new beginning.

John arrives in the city at noon. The mission is to kill a prominent lawyer who is also a businessman. He's a man who is already picked to lead the Conservative Party, and he's outstanding. He's easy to kill because he doesn't know if he's on a hit list. John was already informed that the lawyer is supposed to give a conference in the afternoon at a Hotel downtown Toronto. John plans to kill him when his car stops at a light. The problem remains that the car has shaded windows.

The lawyer's car is circulating on the streets in downtown Toronto. He's sitting on the left side with somebody else on his right. The lawyer's driver is not a bodyguard. John parks his car ahead of them and walks down the street. As the vehicle stops at the light, he pulls out two automatic pistols and empties them by the window where the lawyer is sitting. He's screaming as John starts running while leaving the two weapons on the ground. John takes the cab and goes further up from the downtown area. He shops a little bit and takes the bus to Montreal.

He's now a champ in all the sense of the word. Is John dreaming about the day when he won't have to kill anyone? The answer would be: negative because of his foot on every footstep left by Pepper. He's an efficient blind follower. John is lucky to be the perfect gang member, a good soldier who likes the deadly tranches and ready to sacrifice his life for his bodies and his country. Every experienced military knows perfectly how dangerous one of their members can be by the strict obedience of all rules. Only Pepper or Ann can stop John. He never holds on for a second and to tries be conscious of what he's doing. Some people are crawling doing things like John. Him, he has the natural talent to accomplish maybe the worst and the most challenging job on earth which is to execute killing contracts. He never shows any remorse like he hates human beings and loves to punish them.

The six years that separated him and Ann didn't matter at all. In that short period that they restarted to see each other, they're already very close. She's coming to his house after talking to him on the phone.

"Where were you? I repeatedly called at the office, and you weren't there."

"I stepped out to go do something. Don't worry... now I'm there..."

"John, honey, tell me what's going to happen to us in the next years or so... I want to know."

"I guess, I hope that we'll get married. You said that you loved me and I felt that you are somebody who I can spend my life with."

"John, I can see the attachment that you feel towards me... but I'm wondering, you can't tell me that you love me... Come on, say it: I love you, Ann McIntosh..."

It's already time for another felony. John is a busy man who has many delicate things to do. Ann wouldn't be able to understand. This time, he's in the Old Montreal area - a quite calm place for crimes. John has two legal suitcases containing $5 million. He has to take possession of a big shipment of heroin from an Asian dealer that nobody trust. The WESTSIDE-CONS have some other regular people who are in charge to make exchanges. Pepper gives this exchange to John because it's unique and it's an excellent occasion to make some profits. He's very nervous because it's not about killing somebody. In his mind, he feels that he doesn't have any control over the situation.

John is near the rails waiting for the Asian gang whose bringing the precious heroin. Again he's utterly alone with no backup. The Asian posse is walking near the track. They're at least twelve guys. John uses a cell phone to call the chief as a sign that he's the right person who is carrying the money. The gang leader is advancing toward

John with three members holding the shipment. John gives him one suitcase so he can see the money as he's verifying the quality of the heroin. He gave them the rest of the money as they do the same for the heroin. John is leaving just as they are going with all the money. Suddenly, a member of the gang who was hiding jump close to John as he's threatening him with a pistol at his neck. John drops the shipment on the floor as the pistol of the gangster is at his throat. The man gets distracted a little bit as John takes possession of the gun and shoots the man several times. The rest of the gang pull their weapons to literally spray John with bullets as he luckily takes cover so fast that they miss him. All the group of bandits is still together when John pulls two Israeli Uzi riffles and shoots all of them in a matter of seconds. The entire gang is lying on the floor completely dead. John looks very surprised as he's still pointing his riffles in every possible direction, thinking that some other members are there. He verifies the bodies. They are all dead. John is breathing very fast and thinking that his life is still in danger. Finally, he's leaving with the money and the shipment.

After he walked far enough from the dead bodies, he sees a car with the keys in the ignition. This is what they commonly call a "hot car." He loads everything in the car and leaves. John is driving east. Fifteen minutes after, he stops the car and unloads the shipment and the money. Then takes a cab with the idea to go further east and take another taxi without being seen by the first cab. As the first drop him off, he walks a little bit and picks the second one. Now, he's going straight to his contact in Montreal-North to give him everything like he was told. John gets inside an apartment block and puts the money and the heroine in the second-floor apartment. He takes the bus to the subway and manages to don't go straight home.

From the way John does his crime's actions, it's unquestionably true that the criminals are brilliant and show a lot of intellectual capabilities. In their daily job, they demonstrate the quite difficult to keep going safely and successfully. It's not strange that he's a professional criminal just like he's a magistrate. The only troubling thing is that people who are civil officers are trusted to be morally impeccable. Looking at John, it's logic to think that many dark secrets are not revealed, which is the reason why there is trust all over the societies. For John, none of the ethical things that exist are important to him, right now.

The next day, while driving on Highway 40, he calls Pepper. It's already night time, and many planes are in the skies. There are very hard noises from the reactors. He's not bothered at all. It's the West Island area. The phone is ringing. He's driving faster like he was testing some engine like an automobile racing pilot. After all, it's a brand new Porsche, it needs to be pushed over the speed limit, just like on the 'Autobahn' in Germany.

"Hello! John..."

"Yeah... It's me... How are you man..."

"Fine. Fine. Nice to hear from you... Did everything went well?"

"Yes, but not like expected. I had to waste all these bastards. Can you believe that they tried to kill me and keep everything."

"Nice, nice... Don't worry you man, you did what you had to do. I mean Lung-Ming never give a damn about any justice or whatever... It's always the same thing with him... you're a hero now... I want you to meet me at my place - it's critical!"

In the last days, five to be precise, John kills as many as eight persons and more. Now, some alarm signal just rings in his mind because Pepper wants to see him for something important. It took John fifteen minutes to get to Pepper's house. Pepper is waiting outside as John parks in front of the house. It seems to John that Mary is not there. Pepper embarks in John's car and tells him to make a turn back in the other direction. John finds him strange because his head is continually turning like he's watching out for something.

"That's a new car? You just bought it..."

"Yeah. Two days ago. Actually, I rent it..."

"FInd. Relax man... I know what you've been thru for the last days, but some other crucial things to do. We must waste the S.C.R.S. director. He's our main target now... okay..."

When they arrive at the house, Mary is in the shower. They're heading downstairs in Pepper's office to talk business.

"Mary! Where are you darling? I'm home."

"I'm under the shower! What took you so long?"

"Nothing. I'm going to be downstairs with John if you need me."

"Pepper man, why the Canadian secret service director? Are you nuts man?"

"Nope, I have all my mind. He's responsible for the Laurentians destruction. If we don't eliminate him now, we won't exist anymore. To tell you the truth, he's working for his own people just like us. It's not a question of justice, it's a challenge."

"Business as usual; I'll get him myself just like the other ones."

"Oh no, we'll be together this time. Don't forget that when we kill this idiot, all his subordinates will disappear with him. If we miss, we can suicide ourselves because he will certainly get us and we won't have the chance to kill him anymore."

"Fine, it's like you want. I'll follow you."

Most of the people who are working at the head of the Canadian government live in Suburban Ottawa. And the S.C.R.S. director is one of them. Pepper and John are well prepared to send him to his grave. Somebody must be thinking that they should have done the same thing to Hoover of the FBI. The two experienced bandits are very careful because some men are so lucky when comes the time to die.

The Canadian secret service director is getting out of his car as his bodyguards are observing.

The director is out of the car, and he's sauntering towards the door. John and Pepper are coming in a car, they stop right in front of the house and pull their machine guns to spray everybody with bullets. They set the entire place on fire with explosive and grenades in a matter of seconds as they quickly leave by helicopter. As he gets out of the chopper to take a car, he talks to an agent who is well informed about the secret services.

"The agency will burn all his files. Nobody ever trusts that director. He's too corrupt. So, there won't be anything left on you. It will be like they've known nothing about you."

"So I can use my contacts now to delete all the files."

"Affirmative. For all the police corps, you never existed with no records."

Now, it's like their criminal life was over once for all. They've eliminated probably all the people that could stop them from going where they want in life. WESTSIDE-CONS is well established and strong as they've earned the respect of the crime community. John is now leading a quite vast and troubling organization that will probably kill two to five thousand persons for one year only. The waste product of a gang like theirs is similar to the toxicity and the after effect of the cocaine that they sold. Why don't people consume procaine or novocaine? The two substitutes and synthesis products of cocaine are medically used as painkilling because of their safety. John feels well for the reason that people can know all that they wish to make good use of the things that are accessible to them. Would there be a problem with the feelings? Mean, they will take something that makes them feel good even if the risks are high. So, John is not different because of his knowledge, for the reason that he's looking forward to his glory and the most increasing wealth possible - no matter the danger as significant as it could be. After Pepper talked to the agent, hestops his car by a little park in Downtown Ottawa like he's having a break. It's time to chat with John.

"You never told me that it was our last mission. It's not our job anymore to kill people."

"You got it! "BLASTER" is getting out of prison very soon to replace me. We will just have to take care of the companies and the investments. I'll be able to look at Mary and Ann in the eyes because the lies are over."

"Yeah. You must be right... Ann told me that I'm stern and mysterious... She also told me that when I say something nice, my face doesn't look like it. Man! It had to be that killing job. It's almost impossible to be in love with your wife and be a gangster..."

"Don't a soft man... The last easy-going thing in the world is a woman. Put your stuff together with Ann and get back to business. If we keep going, this entire world will be ours very soon."

And, it is time to take their goals more seriously. They know what to do at every step because John is well informed about almost anything. There are public relations firms which are a great help to anybody that wish to occupy some very high governmental positions. It's not a joke that John and Pepper would do a good deal by doing business with them.

John is meeting a public relations specialist in Montreal to evaluate his potential to rise up at the commanding positions in the Canadian government. Pepper is doing the same thing at the other end in an office in Manhattan.

"I mean you're twenty-six years old - you got plenty of time in front of you. We can work out your relations carefully for the next ten to fifteen years, and you'll certainly become the president of the U.S.A."

"You're sure about that? Me, President..."

"You better believe it... Your turn as president in ten to fifteen years is assured."

"You're twenty-two years old... Give yourself some time, in ten to fifteen years from now, you'll be Prime Minister of Canada. During that time, we'll manage your relations..."

"You must be kidding... Me, Prime Minister of Canada..."

"Oh yes! Without a doubt... You will become Prime Minister just like death and taxes...

The scientists of the world should start working seriously to clarify a specific general rule of optimization. In such a law, somebody would read that if a man can live partially happy for twenty years with twenty-one thousand dollars, he will surely have a paradise with one million dollars. That's precisely the situation of John, right now. After collecting all those millions, he's presently at a satisfied peak of wealth. He's thinking about gathering his people around him to be at the top of all wealth and power. John calls a big dinner at his uncle's house in T.M.R. Everybody is present, and they're talking. Ann and John are almost on one chair, and they never lose an occasion to kiss each other. They don't seem to be preoccupied with what has been said.

"Uncle Ken, you know that a public relation agent told me the other day that I will become Prime Minister of Canada by the next ten to fifteen years. He guaranteed it..."

"I certainly hope something like that for you... but..."

"There is no but... uncle Ken. My companies are doing very well. And, there is absolutely nothing that I ignore. I've been offered all kinds of position...lawyer, Vice-President..."

"You didn't do any post-secondary education... did you graduate in law or administration?"

"No... my dear uncle..." He touches his uncle's shoulder. "I was smart enough to do all the things that lead to the possession of everything... I have a lot of cash..."

"John, you certainly have a lot of money, but you should think about some other thing than power... all these things that are very demanding... I'm not going to marry some guy that can never be home..."

"Power or not, people like John can't stay home for an entire week. Most of those male college graduates... or John... always manage to don't be home... And, they rarely have their only beloved wife... There is still a mistress somewhere..."

"Me, I think that my cousin is too straight for that kind of things. Look at him... he looks so good with Ann that nothing will separate them."

"John is a nice man... You're probably right... because Nixon's wife never agreed his political appointments... It's too much for anybody... not for the man only..."

John and Ann are still kissing voraciously.

"It's all a question of greatness... Any man that has to occupy some very high position is by nature a casual and abnormal husband. These men rarely marry anybody. I mean Eleanor, Coretta, Jackie, are far away from ordinary people - they had their destiny to..."

"Anyway, dinner is always an occasion to hear some quite unbelievable stories... My dear John, I'll believe you when I see you in the Parliament... Although I wish you sincerely to reach your every goal." Many social events are never part of our thoughts. The reason is simple. It's pure logic. A smart man think of getting married when he feels that he's rich enough. On the opposite, a stupid individual wants to tie the knots as soon as he knows that he's in love. They're both losers with their estimations that the best mathematician wouldn't approve. Naturally, on a beautiful day of October, Ann and John conveymany people at their wedding. The priest is presenting the vows. After saying yes on both sides, they kiss. The best men and the entire group are leaving the church. John is wearing an Ascot tie, and Ann has a lovely beautiful dress.

John and Ann are in England for their honeymoon. They're featured in the Hempel Zen Garden. Actually, they're walking hand in hand, and they're enjoying the beautiful garden. Their photograph is making pictures of them as they're walking. They embark in their automobile in the direction of Kensington Palace. John meets the Queen and the royal family. Ann knew that he. They spend the night at the Palace.

The next day, a beautiful morning, they're heading Downing Street to go meet the Prime Minister. When they arrive at the Prime

Minister's house, in a matter of minutes, several journalists are there to photograph John and Ann. In all, their daily visit to Britain is like a dream. Everything is terrific, the places that they see, the people they meet and the press coverage. The nights they spend making love with their quite big hunger for sex.

Indeed, the nuptial thing and all that comes with it makes a therapeutic effect on a criminal like John. It's another lie of human beings to think that a successful criminal who succeed get married with his riches instead of getting caught and go suffer in prison. A little bit of common sense would induce to think that winning is the best therapy. Indeed, John is happy. Now, six months after their honeymoon in Britain, he's in his personal house sitting in the back near the patio with Ann who is already pregnant. Actually, she already has a big belly. John jumps in the swimming pool as he's mocking himself of her who's a little bit paralyzed by her pregnancy.

Substantially, nothing has changed in human life in general. The same cycle keeps its pace as it's repeating itself. Nobody would know if it's boring to get married and have kids along with a good career and a certain level of wealth to be able to live somewhat decently. Something interesting is not boring at all. Maybe a good knowledge of science which shows so many aspects that anything, such as marriage and family life can take, will undoubtedly change the mind. Some old rituals would look too ancient and out of style. Again, John doesn't have time and probably never thought of kind of things like that. His style is the tie, the suitcase, the business, the cash, the vacations, and Ann. Later, the kids will be there too.

He didn't have to wait because several months already passed and Ann is having contractions. John is rushing from his business travel in Vancouver to be there before she gives birth. All the nurses and the doctor are close to Ann preparing themselves to help her deliver the child. She's showing a painful face when pushing under the chief-nurse instructions. The baby gets out, and they bring it to her.

Then, they cut the umbilical cord and take the baby away from her. John just arrives, and he's touching Ann's face and make sure she's doing very well. He sits close to her and holds her neck by him while he's telling her that he loves her.

It's been three years since the first baby. Now, there are two more. The residential streets of Montreal are John's favorite place to walk with his kids. He has to become a father at his turn by taking care of the kids once in a while as a symbol for the future generations. John and Ann are walking with their two babies. One of the children is three, and the other is ten months. It's a beautiful sunny day. He must be thinking what all this means apart from the usual task of the humans that exist to reproduce themselves for the conservation of the species. There are other things. He thinks that it gets to be a theological matter. No, he replied in his mind: the reason is that everything he has in his imagination can be real.

A good example is the planes that fly very fast. Before there were those powerful flying cars, some idiot has probably thought it would be impossible. For John, the idea of never dying and play forever with Ann and his kids are the first preference. Similarly, many stupid people don't believe in the possibility of such a thing. Another time, John would admit for sure that an intelligent man like himself will devote his entire life asking or looking at non-responded questions. That's a better way?

Life is lovely for John because another summer comes at the residence in Peggy's Coves, Nova Scotia. He's with Pepper walking in the big yard of the house. The noises of their kids playing near the pool can be heard from afar. Ann and Mary just double up to join them.

"You like the garden? The flowers are nice, but there are no roses."

"Why don't you get a Bonsai... This is a real funny plant. I mean a Japanese garden is good... compare to..."

"We should have a garden like that. I surely wouldn't keep taking care of it myself..."

"Mary, you see the bird... It's a Martin... At this time of the year, there are a lot of birds..."

"It's very nice."

"I would like to see an eagle. There is none around here. Next time we should go on vacation in Africa, like Kenya, Congo. I really want to see a lot of animals like elephants, snakes, in their real-life habitat."

His parents, Bill and Margaret, are getting out of their car. John and Ann are walking toward them.

"Oh, my son, John - as John hug both parents together. You must be having a good time here. Everything is so beautiful. That's the first time you came here since you bought that house. My God... I'll come here more often..."

"You guys seem to be in good shape... How is Aunt Martha? I'm going to call her, later on, to see if she can come to join us."

"Margaret, come with me!" - as she takes her harm and gets closer." I got something to show you." The new dresses that she just bought.

"Oh my God! It's wonderful! When did you get them?"

They're going to the bedroom. John's mother is helping Ann to undress and try the new outfits. She compliments Ann as she's looking in the mirror.

"Ann! Where are you?"

"I'm in the room upstairs! Come up."

John walks up the stairs and gets into the room and come face to face with Ann and her new dress.

"Darling, you look wonderful. Is that the dress that you just got?"

"Yeah. The clothes are very nice. I'll probably order my dresses in the future from the same designer."

"You know that Kenneth will come here with Isabelle and Yvonne.

Every single member of this family..."

"They're about to come here... My God!...anyway, there are so many rooms here..."

In the evening, two cars are pulling in the parking. Mr. Kenneth Barlow, his daughters and their husbands and aunt Martha. John, his father, and mother along with Ann, walk out to come to see them.

"We wanted to surprise you. It worked... hey!"

"Actually, your mouths must have slipped because mummy just told me that your guys were coming. Next time, make sure you don't tell anybody at all..."

"Aunt Margaret! It was a secret..."

"Oh! I completely forgot," she showed that she purposely told John about their arrival.

They're at least eighteen family members on the patio and the large yard of the house. The kids are playing frisbee. Some of them are in the swimming pool. Everybody is up to something fun and informal. John is walking with Ann and Pepper while Mary is kind of playing kid's game, flapping their hands with Isabelle. Suddenly, a car is coming toward the house. John knows that it's William, his right arm political advisor. And he thinks that something extraordinary must have come up. Now, John is walking toward William who is about to park.

"William man! How are you? I thought you would be in Montreal."

"I'm fine. Fine!" William is very excited. " I have good news: the chief of the Liberal Party of Canada Is Interested In you to run In the N-D-G riding. Not only that, a lot of important people are looking at you to lead the party someday. You can start thinking about your agenda."

"Where did you get all that? I mean, I was expecting good news but nobody contacted me..."

William and John enter the house. They're going in the living room. We can hear their boisterous conversation with their high voices.

Now, John and Wesley are more preoccupied rising to power than to do anything constructive. Their wealth kept on growing to some gigantic proportions. People still can't really say that they didn't do anything good for the world because money corrupted them. It's because of life becomes miserable without the CASH - and that creates some kind of a financial obsession.

He began to travel all over the country to meet people and talk to them. John went to Sudbury, Sarnia, Etobicoke, Mississauga, Regina, Calgary and to several cities in British Colombia. He mostly spoke to the same kind of people: Mayors, Deputies, CEO's, Vice-Presidents, Rectors, Columnists, authors, actors, and actresses. They invite him to a lot of regional TV shows.

Whatever he does he always make sure people know Wesley too.

"Mr. Barlow, what part of the country you like best?" A talk show host in Vancouver asked him.

"Dartmouth, Nova Scotia, that's where I'm originally from. To tell you the truth, I really like it." John told Juliet Powell.

"You mean you don't prefer the nice weather in Vancouver." She told him with a joking face.

"No... No... I don't mean that..."

"So... Tell us... We wanna know..." Juliet Powell said as she laughs.

"Hum... Huh... Vancouver is nice, but I'm a Nova-Scotian. It's just like that... And I'm an African-Canadian... We've always lived there... It's our place," John replied.

Usually, Juliet Powell works in Toronto. She went to Vancouver for a month to replace some friends that went to Nigeria. John would have probably declined the invitation if it wasn't the beautiful and intelligent Juliet. It's perhaps the only real moral in John's life: he honors everything that looks black. And the secret behind his success is that nobody ever knew they were doing business with him. Although he could have used the fact that he's a racially mixed person. And these people can easily pass for a white - their two-faced is not successful in the black community.

For some reason, John had the impression during his travels around the country that the population would trust a gentleman like him. He seems to be very focused on his goals. Almost everything in his life is clear or well defined. From his experience and thorough knowledge about anything, he is assured that he knows how to govern these nine thousand square kilometers and its thirty-seven thousand people. He feels that it's essential to don't let anyone knows about his atheism. John doesn't ignore the fact that a man who doesn't believe in God shouldn't be at the head of a country. The simple idea of just managing the resources to make life more enjoyable for the citizens is incomplete - although it is the central part of an atheist conception of life.

It took two years before Pepper and John return to the summer residence in Peggy's Cove, Nova Scotia. They didn't think it would be their last time going there. John's wife still ignores everything about WEST SIDE-CONS with the illegal activities that are the usual components of gangs.

"What do you think Pepper about all these religious blah... blah.." John asked.

"Me I know that I got baptized just like a standard procedure... and not because I believe in whatsoever...," Pepper said.

Ann is looking closely at both of them as Pepper's wife Mary is playing with Ben and Jessica. John's wife is a great believer who would explain her faith without trying to convince anybody. Actually, her religious knowledge is more than excellent.

"I think you should start asking God for his blessings in your everyday activities. What do you think John?" Ann was talking to John and Pepper only.

"Of course... we will Ann," John and Pepper answered.

In fact, they've always answered favorably to their wives and most undoubtedly affirmative in the case of a theological suggestion like this one. Without being sexist, they seem to think that only women take religion seriously. For John, if his wife would ask him to quit these criminal activities, he would undeniably agree with the risk of being purged internally. It's dangerous for John to have a wife like Ann and a friend like Pepper at the same time. John and his wife can cause the gang to break apart with all its relations. Pepper knows that a long time ago, but for some reason, he never told John. According to the unwritten rules of criminal gangs, John can't leave WESTSIDE-CONS.

"Have you ever think to let someone else lead WESTSIDE-CONS? I mean you'll get a position as CEO - you won't be able to lead the two."

"Actually I'm always thinking about keeping everything under my control. Unless you wanna piece... I don't know..."

"No. I was just thinking about the efficiency of our stuff... You know what I mean..."

"I know what you mean... But I'll tell there are none of our guys capable of keeping WESTSIDE-CONS business in a good position... So if you wanna piece... I'll give you a piece for sure... because you can do business," Pepper said that like a conclusion of their conversation.

Pepper still thinks that John wasn't experienced enough in conducting illegal business although he has a lot of talent. After all, the gang form an army of several thousand members - plus two to three times cadet-members. The expansion prediction is sixty percent increase in size every year for the next three years. Right now the gross asset of WESTSIDE-CONS is many billion dollars. They have more weapon than the Canadian Armed Forces. The violence capacity and the economic strength of some North-American gangs is so impressive that the governments forbid the institutions to make a clear account or any real report. The unwritten policy is to keep them calm. Also, since people like John and Pepper are controlling a gang, it is considered that there is nothing to worry about.

Pepper falls asleep on the patio couch. Mary and Ann have an excellent discussion. John is reading the Globe and Mail and a novel by Farley Mowat. Actually, he brought five books for the summer: he's trying to finish the third part of Leviathan by Thomas Hobbes (Of a Christian commonwealth) ; Lady Chatterley's Lover by D.H. Lawrence ; The Red Thread by Montrealer Nicholas Jose ; Smother Love by Irena F. Karafilly. As summer rolled in that beautiful Maritimes part of Canada, a scorching wind is crossing Peggy's Cove just like the Harmattan blows in West-Africa from December to February.

It is time for supper: roasted chicken with pepper sauce. Like in all wealthy families everything is being done smoothly. Do rich politicians really live in a tense period while an election is going on? We'll never know. Anyway, Ben and Jessica are having fun playing with the food in some kind of a theatrical style. Alice is laughing with Ann, pulling her mom's cheek with her small hands and rubbing her nose against her's. Pepper's two sons Jesse and Alex are playing Nintendo.

During the vacations, it doesn't look like there is another world where people are working - carrying, lifting, buying, bargaining, phoning. The Kemps and the Barlows were having some real vacations. Since it is business as usual in Montreal specially and because of some significant transactions going on, it's always possible for Pepper to receive a call.

There are twenty-five members of WESTSIDE-CONS on vacation with Pepper. It is categorically not easy to move around with all these people. A gang is more a burden than a former business staff.

Pepper still wants to get out of all this. He thinks he was happier before. John told him that it was normal to feel that way in the beginning. He doesn't know that it is the strong desire of Pepper to put him in charge of everything. There is no way for them to understand that some sad moments are ahead of them.

"Things are getting nasty over here man. Two new gangs want to take our place. I want your permission to spray them," a Route-Sergeant of WESTSIDE-CONS calling from Montreal told Pepper.

"Yeah. Just smoke all these people and pretend that there was a third one and do the same," Pepper told the man on the phone.

The problems of Pepper are more significant than he would think. Fanengen's crew is all over the three provinces: Quebec, Ontario, and British Colombia. For some reason, criminality revenues are flourishing around the big Canadian cities, and a lot of other influential people want their part. It goes from Russian-Mob to Yakusas - a lot of people =they're now playing American half-court basketball. It's hard to imagine the level of violence that is about to take place. The territory is small, and everybody is well armed - nobody wants to share anything - or to negotiate anything. Usually, Pepper would have returned to Montreal, his home-base to take care of business. But he really has enough. The idea of a gang sounds like a non-sense. He still has the potential and the energy, but he feels like some other duties are calling him. He's been thinking that criminality isn't supposed to be a permanent occupation. It looks smart to dump WESTSIDE-CONS and keep the CASH for him and John.

A cab came to pick up the kids to a hotel in Halifax. Pepper figured out that by night time he and John should be able to escape forever. Of course, John agreed that it was time to leave the gang business. It's not a question of moral. They're still cheaters who are merely changing the direction of their business.

Pepper will have a new identity. Fanengen will never find him. His departure was planned a long time ago. All his personal belongings and the essential papers were at a location unknown to anybody. That's only Pepper's perception - the excellent protection that he has. In a way, it is fair to say that when you let the group down, you will eventually go down. Or like people use to tell: "What goes around comes around." From that, we can say that a gang is a brotherhood for life. The ones who quit will pay the price. All the people that want Pepper knows a lot of things about him. Actually, they know everything about him.

CHAPTER 4

Brant "Pepper" Kemp has a new name which is Wesley Bradford. He's the CEO of Devon Network Telecom that has its Head office in Montreal. John was elected Deputy in NDG where he presently lives. Both Wesley and John are on their way to the highest governmental positions in Ottawa. As a criminal, John seems to have learned a lot from that ignominious status. The journalists know well enough how much he cherishes the concept of Welfare Economics, not as normative micro-economics, but as a generalization of the government's welfare programs. It's safe to know that a cheater like John is not a right-wing politician - Bradford also. They all have progressive ideas.

The four months gang war was disastrous. As the members of WESTSIDE-CONS were falling down under the bullets of enemy gangs, Bradford could read it sadly in the papers. By the moment, he felt like going back to help them. The problem is that he acquired too much wisdom during the years and he became like incapable of making stupid decisions. And it appears clearly that it's not logic that is supposed to be the primary basis of our choices - but opportunity. Was it logic for Bradford to abandon his companions in the middle of a gang war?

"Hey, West! there's a big dinner at Finance Minister official residence this Friday. I think you should be there. Everybody will be there. Actually, all the people that we need are on the list," John was calling from his deputy office on Cavendish Blvd in Cote-St-Luc.

"Yeah man, make sure I am on the list. Why don't you pick me up at my place early in the day."

"Yeah! Yeah man! That sounds good. You know... Treasury secretary Rubin... Allan Greenspan... Canadian Bank Governor... IMF President... United Nations... It's a damn good one..."

The main reason why John was happy about the dinner is that he already knows most of these extraordinary people. And they find him attractive. He basically wants to get closer to them and tests the viability of his economic ideas. A prominent Economist, Mr. Julius Robertson already sent a report to John stating that the concept of Welfare Economics fits very well in any chief of State agenda - only the infrastructure and the implementation need to be developed. Mr. Robertson makes a comparison with some public things that are, and people just go get them as they need to.

In his preparation to climb at the head of the Liberal Party, John knows that he shouldn't undermine the religious leaders. He's already in contact with his cousin Isabelle who is married to a Pastor, Rev. Troy Wilson, who is leading a congregation of Protestant churches along with some other Christian groups? John puts Wilson in charge of placing him and Wesley in this challenging political terrain. In a way, John is fortunate because Rev. Troy Wilson is some kind of a Jesse Jackson or Martin Luther-king Jr. - very religious believer - also brilliant tactically and strategically to play the poker game of POLITICS.

Now Rev. Wilson makes sure a lot of pastors quote John's name in almost every sermon. The Reverend has a lot of friends beyond the Catholic priests. Wilson already talked to some Islamic and Judaist representatives about John's neutrality and diplomatic ideas about the conflictual situation of the two groups. He can go see any religious group - his image is excellent in front of them.

Mrs. Wilson - John's cousin Isabelle is currently completing her Master's degree in Law at McGill University. She's very close to John, and it would be a good idea to use her skills and contacts. John called her for a supper invitation at a Caribbean restaurant.

"So where you up to, sister. I mean you're always thinking about cousin John," he said with a smile. "Are you about to become Judge Isabelle, the one who is going to punish John for his sins... or reward him no matter what he does..."

"I'm doing fine. Like you know I love my husband a lot... And I'm looking forward to becoming a Judge one of these days. Of course, I will reward my cousin all the time... no matter what," Isabelle said.

"Someday, I want to be the PM of Canada. Do you think it's possible? I'm just not too sure about my Politico-economical agenda... Are you familiar with the concept of Welfare Economics?" John is talking to her like he's in love.

"Nope, I don't know anything about Welfare Economics...," she is holding his left hand by crossing his fingers with her's as she states: "Johnny-baby, my dear cousin if it's not the Law, I don't know anything about it. Law is all I know. Actually, I'm so good that I can make anything looks lawful."

Indeed, if Reverend Wilson could read John and Isabelle's mind, he would have married them instead of marrying her. Ann knows that perfectly well, and that's for why he married John. She couldn't understand how two persons who are so attracted to each other never consciously decided to be together. There's better than that, uncle Ken knows that old love-story that never died. How come Reverend Wilson never suspected that?

Troy Wilson is a Reverend just like another person would be a biologist. Wilson also thinks that John is the kind of guy who has respect for the basic rules of religion and civilization... And we all know that John is a criminal... For some reason, we tend to think that somebody can keep on doing bad things and remain the right person. Uncle Ken, Bill, and Margaret and some other close people have at least a slight idea of John illegal and dangerous activities.

After the waiter put all the food on the table, Isabelle looked at John as she smiled at the same time. She makes a sign for John to approach his face closer to hers. As John got closer, she told him: "can I kiss you on the lips?" John is about to ask her why, but the temptation is too much. He kisses her generously along with all the touching that always goes on between two lovers. She's living the best moments of her life. It' a perfect combination because the Reverend is travelling in the US and their two kids are over uncle Ken's place.

As John's driver gets in front of the Reverend's house, he wants to stop everything thereby not entering the house. Isabelle is in his arms with the left side of her face against his chest. They are hooked, and they can't leave each other. John gets out of the Lincoln Continental, and he enters the house. He tells his driver to go.

They spent the night together hoping that it would be some kind of a one-night-stand in the mid-life period of their existence. No, It wasn't. They slept for five days in the same bed. Of course, they both had to lie to their partners. And, destroying news came to them on television and on the phone. At the bottom of the screen of channel twenty-five, a flashing message says: "NEWS UPDATE," CANADIAN PASTOR TROY WILSON WAS SHOT IN ALLENDALE PENSYLVANIA FOR AN UNKNOWN REASON. And then, Carla Robinson presents the news by saying: "Montrealer Reverend Troy Wilson was shot this morning in Allendale Pennsylvania while he was about to close a seven-day revival in the US. The Reverend was shot two times in the head from what is believed to be a large caliber weapon. We have a report from NBC Sandra Hughes.

"Reverend Troy Wilson came in the US to conduct a seven-day revival. The first day he went to Eben-Ezer Baptist Church in Atlanta Georgia where people gathered to listen to the "true prophet of God" who was delivering an eloquent message that touched deeply almost everybody who was present. Then he went to churches in California, Arkansas, Louisiana, Mississippi, Florida and here in Pennsylvania where he received the two fatal bullets. All that leaves the friends of the Reverend in a complete stupor because he is not known to have enemies that would want to assassinate him. Reverend Troy Wilson is not part of any underworld activity. The case is now in the hand of a special group of detectives formed by the FBI under the command of (DA) Attorney Janet Reno. The President felt very uncomfortable that renown and respected evangelical Minister was murdered on US soil. Sandra Hughes, NBC news, Allendale, Pennsylvania." The news anchor reaches Sandra Hughes live to ask her some questions about the assassination:

"Can you describe the conditions in which the Reverend was killed?" Carla Robinson asked.

"All we know Carla is that the Reverend was coming out of the Marriot Hotel where he spent the night, and we saw his head popped off two times. Since he doesn't have bodyguards because nobody expected that he would be attacked. So, when all that happened, the people surrounding the Reverend were trying to protect themselves and him."

"Did the FBI already came up with something on who might have committed such a crime against the Reverend?"

"They make several arrests, but they still didn't announce any possible links with the assassination. There's the hypothesis of a hate group that was put down. Also, the success story of Reverend Wilson wife's family that could have been the envy of some jealous people. In conclusion, we can say that nothing is clear yet," Sandra finally answered.

"Thank you, Sandra... Keep us up to date on any new development." Bye... Bye...," Carla Robinson concluded her News Update.

There we are, Reverend Troy Wilson is one of these smart guys that knows what to do even if they're never careful enough. He gave a good boost to his career as Reverend by marrying Isabelle Barlow. It is evident that the Barlows have a lot of strength even though there are a lot of holes in their business. There's probably no safe place for somebody that is hanging around with the ex-Pepper and has some old relation with a gang like the WESTSIDE-CONS. By being very intelligent and well known, the Reverend posed a violent threat to anybody that would want the death of John and Wesley. It looks like the men of God are always in a weak position when they're looking for the glory of this world.

Isabelle was shocked by the news. She knows the strength of her cousin John and thought maybe he could have done something to protect her husband. He couldn't do anything at all. Now he has the sign that he better defends himself and Wesley.

Now, John went to his uncle's house right after the news of the assassination. He knows very well that Mr. Kenneth Barlow doesn't trust him as a sincere man. Why? John always thought that people like his uncle simply never believe an extremely wealthy individual like himself - especially when it's a direct family member. Mr. Kenneth Barlow probably feels that it's a big mystery for him to know how one man can gather several billions of dollars. He just can't understand something like that even if he's a business graduate. After all, people that are very rich come from any discipline. Maybe John would make an effort to tell his uncle with a little bit of philosophical talent that everybody steals. In the sense that there is no real difference between human beings with the exception that some people are more opportunistic than others. And if everyone has a salary, many will find a way to take a part of that paycheck to put on theirs. Everything is available to each of us just like water.

Obviously, uncle Ken is like these men for whom the castles in Spain will always be fictitious. He ignores the extent of his nephew's opulence. Looking at a man like John's uncle, we would tend to think that traditions are not that effective. It's time to throw out the old ideas, even the biblical ones in the garbage. In any successful kid, there is some kind of disobedience. John certainly never did anything else than questioning the whole parenthood fears to impose definite illegal ideas.

"I feel sad for what happened to Troy. Who would want to kill him? After all, Troy is not...," John didn't finish his phrase that his uncle replied right away.

"You should tell me. These companies and businesses of yours seem very strange to me."

"Uncle Ken, I'm a very successful businessman... There's absolutely nothing strange in what I do. If I were doing doubtful stuff, these bullets would have hit me."

"Hum... Humm... Who asks Troy to help to gather the churches for your political goals? There is something in there..."

"If Troy was shot because I asked him to help to do my campaign, it certainly not me who's doing strange business. Uncle Ken, I really don't understand those kinds of speculation. You think that I have something to do with Troy's assassination... Is this real?"

Maybe, uncle, Ken is right about the dark secrets that lie under all extreme wealth. John doesn't care that much because he's not at fault. Some people are just too emotional to look closely at things like they are and face them. The world itself is a mix of ten percent of people who are focused and ninety percent of undisciplined people. Anybody that is walking around energizing humans like Troy was doing is a little bit lost mentally. The Gospel is very personal, and there is no way to make it down this earth by socializing too much. When you're not very well paid to do something, it's intelligent to don't do anything. Nobody has an idea of the market value of a famous Reverend like Troy Wilson. What else can you encounter when you're selling good things like the Gospel at no charge?

Looking at Ann, we can say that John has the wife that goes with his big fortune. She behaves like the perfect wife, and John has the courage of a husband. An image is the most important thing on earth: we should never look at what we're not supposed to see. There is a multimillion dollar bank-robber who has the tie of a successful businessman and a high-level civil officer. Indeed, the real professional will become a false one. Ann loves John forever. The idea of an accomplished man is very classical. Modernity brought some unprofessional and unaccomplished men with lousy social life. In such a case, there are no more women.

"Ann! I gotta talk to you darling" She takes him with both arms on the hips. "Honey, can you believe that uncle Ken is trying to link my political activities with Troy's death," John mumbled to her.

"Did Troy had something to do with your election? What was his role exactly?"

"Ann, the Reverend is a very effective man. I know that and Isabelle also. So, I simply asked him to gather the support of the religious groups. He got very good at it just before he got killed."

"It's certainly not enough to say that would be the reason why Troy died. Don't worry you about that."

John is like surrounded by two thick, strong metal bars for some kind of protection which are Ann and Pepper. Since his fellow crime partner knows more secrets in his life, their contact can be coldsometimes. John is always trying to rearrange the world or to cure its wounds while Pepper and some other family members are more concerned about the stability of their social standing. It's like in the beginning of the nineteenth century where many aristocrats were driving their cars while some people like John were concerned about finding a way to travel faster or improving the economic condition of the less privileged class of society. Who assign roles to people throughout the world? We don't know. All we see is that some people like Pepper and Ann are very concerned about their wealth and closed ones like John than the problem of the world.

"You heard about the Reverend. I mean, he got shot pretty bad... the killer must have our style," he said swiftly to Pepper.

"This is not the time John. I have to go all the way to South Carolina to receive my honorary rank as colonel. Can we talk about this some other time? I'm in a hurry..."

"You can't come to his funeral... We'll make it in four days, maybe."

"I'll try John! We've been friends for years, man. Most of all, we're brothers... You seem to be sometimes sleeping... you've been playing, talking everywhere about all kinds of economics ideas that are freaking out people... our people, the people that we work so hard to put on our side. I'll be straight with you John. If you still jangling, planning these unrealistic ideas, don't be surprised to see bullets flying all over the place."

"What is it, Pepper? You mean Troy got shot because of my effort to clarify the idea of Welfare Economics. Man, I'll tell you something right now, I'm very close to a way to implement this idea in real life. And, nobody is going to stop me from continuing doing my job!"

"Be careful John! You happen to be a revolutionary... scholar that is in the wrong place at the wrong time. You want to switch everything around! And I can assure you from the information that I got, that none of this is going to happen! You got that man..."

After the death of the Reverend, Isabelle became the mistress of John. Their intimate relationship is not known to nobody. An incestuous son, Albert, was born. Isabelle never told anybody who was the father of the child. It's a secret between her and John.

On the professional front, John became a good friend of the economist, Dr. Julius Robertson. They often met with some other university professors to see the possibility of realizing the idea of Welfare Economics. At the time Dr. Robertson was working on a project to develop a supreme weapon for the Army, so he suggested that John meet Dutch Professor Hans Van Den Doel who already wrote abook called Democracy and Welfare Economics. Before all that, John had some very long discussions about the subject of money with Dr. Robertson.

"It's funny John, I had a friend of mine who was working in the communication department of the CIBC. Actually, his name is Bent Long... We know that the CIBC made a slight change in its logo which was part of a new image program for the bank. I asked Bent to give me an idea of the cost of that image thing... He told me the cost never matters in kind of things like that... The policy is that they always do what they have to do no matter the cost. It's like there is no price in what they do. A good example to understand what's going on exactly in such an institution - if we take a normal consumer like me and you, when we have $100 thousand we can't spend more than that unless we make a loan. In the opposite, these institutions, if they don't have a certain amount, they simply invent it. The amount of money they have is unlimited compared to the limited revenues of the consumer."

"What can the governments do about that?", John replied. "You mean we can't have a closer look in the banks' activities."

"No. It is almost impossible to change these practices. The banks invented money notes or HARD CASH if you prefer. You Know that a long time ago when you would go and make your deposit of gold in a bank, they would increase the number of receipts which are the money notes - the $20-$50-$100 bills that we have now. The real money which is the gold is kept safe protected by five-inch-thick-metal. With such a practice, the banks started to lend money that they don't even have. People never came to claim their gold since today - so these institutions kept flourishing - WELLS FARGO, CHASE MANHATTAN BANK, TD BANK, ROYAL BANK, SCOTIA BANK, NATIONAL BANK..."

"If there is a problem for governments dealing with such an issue, what would be the solution?", John said with a little bit of embarrassment in front of his interlocutor startling revelations.

"It's not to know if there is a problem or not. The issue has always been and remain to find an effective system capable of replacing the dark and mysterious economic practices of capitalism. John Maynard Keynes thought the intervention of governments would be a great solution, but we can clearly see that the same problems as concentration remained. A mixed system like ours in Canada might have sooth a little bit - the miracle is still far."

"Can you inform me a little bit about the viability of Welfare Economics? How it could be implemented?" John asked like some kind of an inquiring journalist.

"First of all, I would like to simplify these big words of "Welfare Economics". It is nothing else than a disguised socialist concept. In other words, the idea must have come from a socialist or a Marxist. Although I won't mention any name... But to continue what I was saying, we know, or we tend to associate Marxist ideas to things that are unrealistic. And there is nothing truer among economist and political scientist that Marxist ideas are mostly dreams. The collapse of the Russian socialist economy illustrates that very well. Also, if it is possible to realize some socialistic ideas like Welfare Economics, that would certainly take a long time."

"What about pretending we have all the resources it would necessitate and we create a huge international entity in collaboration with the UN. Then we produce most of the goods and services that are shipped by airplanes, boats, and train to every country on earth. The populations are provided with a decent salary whether they're working or not."

"It looks to me as an excellent idea. Although I feel like we would need a price policy as a restraint ruling for the number of goods like houses an individual is allowed to possess. There's no doubt that it would be a big mess. Remember how Friedrich von Hayek defines totalitarianism which is "to organize all the society to reach a certain goal."

John worked with another economist to make his economic agenda because some people told him that you don't necessarily need a good program to get the power. He finally realized that real scholars can create a lot of conflict in a group. And instead of economists and other scientists, what he really needs is communication specialist that are always capable of making anything looks good. More important is the friends who are highly placed in the system. A clear analysis of the power components demonstrates that John Barlow could be the next Prime Minister of Canada. Just like some scientists make a lot of money but never make any remarkable or useful discoveries.

In a way, being at the head of a country is the next big step in his life. He ignores all the deep reasons why it's like that and not otherwise.

Beyond all what he ignores, God is indeed there. Is it possible to find why somebody is being chosen to occupy some very high-level position? John doesn't think about any complicate subject or question anymore, he puts all his energy to reach the glorifying position of Prime Minister. He already bought it.

"Hey! Mr. Barlow! How are you?" His neighbor, Mrs. Alain yelled while John was jogging.

"I'm fine! And you? Tell your husband I will call him this evening," John yelled back to her.

"Hi! How you doing?...," the same thing went on during the course of his jogging - people cheering him.

John is now famous in the best sense of the word - to start thinking seriously about his eventual rise to glory in a country where his ancestors came more than three hundred years ago. He knows his history very well as a North-American black person. In general, John likes to minimize these facts. But at this very moment, he started to wake up and learn what he doesn't know.

"Reverend Thompson, how are you?" John called Elijah Thompson to talk to him.

"I'm Fine... Thank God... That makes a long time I didn't see you. You know that you can come down here at any time... Actually, I would like to invite you to Washington... Can you come in three days... Or...," Reverend Elijah Thompson told him in a happy mood.

"Yeah... Yeah... That's a good idea... And since you are the Bibleman, I got some exciting things to ask you," John told the Reverend.

"You know John, I know you for a long time, and it would be my godly pleasure to answer your spiritual questions... Anytime brother...

God loves you, my brother... God loves you... Don't forget that...,"
the Reverend kept on repeating to John.

"I should be in Washington early on Sunday. See you then..." John's
phone kept on ringing at a point that Ann was tired about that.
Friends from all over the country were calling to invite him to parties,
meetings, dinners. There were so many people trying to reach him
that he had to transfer the calls to his office where somebody or the
answering machine would record them.

He already spent some $5 million to promote himself. The
money went mostly to charities. John pays some people directly
sometimes for all kind of things. He never saw somebody that
was honest enough to refuse his CASH. With the years, learned
to pay his way everywhere. Now he's thinking about quitting
that habit.

We're still Friday, September the 2nd 1997- it's 16:30, John just
spoke to Reverend Thompson. He is supposed to supper in about an
hour and then starts reading Democracy And Welfare Economics.
John planned to study Welfare Economics thru a series of about
twelve books: Readings in Welfare Economics, Welfare Economics.
A Liberal Restatement, The Economics of Welfare, Welfare
Economics and Subsidy Programs... The subject itself as normative
microeconomics became a passion for him. He started to think that
he will find a way to make it practical.

Late in the evening, at 21:00, Westley pays him a visit. They talked
for about two hours while Ann and the kids were already sleeping.
He told Wesley about the invitation of Reverend Elijah Thompson
for the beginning of the week. Wesley said that it's a good deal to
meet somebody like the Reverend.

"He's a very nice person to talk to... Hey... I met him three times,
and it was wonderful. He's a strong man in Washington, and he's

on our side. We can call him for anything. Salute him for me when you get there...," Wesley was delighted just hearing about the Reverend.

"Yeah! The Reverend is a good guy. I think it's because of him that I started to question my atheism. A man like Reverend Elijah Thompson is one of the reasons why somebody should believe in God. Let's hope that he will have the time to listen to me...," John is really looking forward to that meeting.

"And... Where you up to this weekend?"

"I'm going to read... It's about developing an economics subject... Yeah!...Welfare Economics... It's not a small one... Even for somebody who knows economics very well - like me..."

"Hum... I've heard about that... There are some who don't like kind of things like that... People like to play with the markets... Keep their steak increasing... And keep on partying endlessly..."

"Me I find it very interesting... And like you know I don't really care about what people don't like..."

"Johnny! Johnny! I just think that you shouldn't lose your mind in stuff like that... It's not business..."

"I know what you mean... Yeah... You might be right..."

"Get the cards man!...Long time didn't play poker. It's time now."

"Yeah... Yeah... West wants to lose... I'll bet you anything You won't win even one game... Just like when we're playing chess...

"You're the wrong man... I won you plenty of times... Keep on dreaming...just like in Michal Jackson's song..."

It often happened that Wesley is dreaming that he would have known John when he was young. He feels like growing up with John have been his best gift. Wesley is fully aware of the situations in life that could change friendship to mutual hatred. For some reason, he was sure that he and John form an unbreakable duet.

After all, people like them are in jail forever - they're out enjoying life at the command positions of society - what a satire!

John woke up on Saturday morning at 08:13, he ate his Rice Krispies with Ben and Alice. Ann was having a good conversation with Jessica while taking care of the plants in the solarium. He makes several calls to some academic friends discussing nothing else than the economy. Conceding the fact that some people show a lot of interest in John's idea of achieving a society with zero financial problems for all members, They don't see how it would be possible to reach such goal and keep everything running. Most countries with a welfare system are not dynamic. Also, the pressure that these countries must apply to keep their population from going to places with liberal economic policy.

Some friends from Ottawa and Stanford University came to his house around supper at 17:15. Among them was Rodrigue Tremblay, a Professor of economics, who John puts in charge to make a report on a logical way to implement a Welfare system. The scholar accepts but he didn't promise anything. Now John is thinking about gathering the thoughts of all these people to realize his project.

At 20:00, he resumes his readings. Then John got his luggage ready to leave early in the morning for Washington. In John's mind, it's not a political trip. But he will discover later on that everything is political.

CHAPTER 5

His Challenger private jet touches the ground at 06:30, another chauffeur was already waiting to drive him at the Four-Season Hotel in downtown Washington. He ate breakfast in his room around 07:30. While eating, his Star-Tac cellular telephone rang. Elijah Thompson welcomes him to Washington and tells him he could come to the Nazarene Baptist Church in suburban Washington, on Jefferson Street. Strangely, John felt like it was the right moment and a good idea to go to the church. At the very moment, some bizarre ideas were crossing his mind. He started to feel deeply embarrassed, shy, ashamed, guilty, sad. John suddenly feels weak, and he rested on the couch for a moment.

At 09:30 he embarked in the Limousine and head to the church. When he arrives in front of the church, he gets out of the car, and a servant leads him to his place. For the first time in his life, John felt really happy singing the Gospel songs. The service was so intense and joyous that it would be false to say that the spirit of God or the former Holly Spirit wasn't present. Then when singing "Amazing Grace," he fell in love with the song along with most of the Protestant Church's songs. And something new came in his life - although he's not sure of what it was precisely - he assumes that it is the God of the heavens and the earth.

Reverend Elijah Thompson feels very good, and he thinks God is with him like he has never been. The Reverend who was conducting the service passes the wireless microphone unto Reverend Thompson. And, he started his sermon calmly by inviting the assembly to read the 12th chapter in the Book of Daniel - verses one and two in the

King James version of the Bible. "And at that time shall Michael stand up, the great prince which standeth for the children of thy people: and there shall be a time of trouble, such as never was since there was a nation even to that same time: and at that time thy people shall be delivered, every one that shall be found written in the book. And many of them that sleep in the dust of the earth shall awake, some to everlasting life, and some to shame and everlasting contempt.

After reading the two verses himself with his usual charming prophetic voice, he suggested the 21st verse of chapter ten. Reverend Thompson emphasizes the words saying "Michal, your prince..." Then Reverend Elijah Thompson preached so loud that listen to him gives the impression of a rock concert. "Brother and sisters, we need leaders,...leaders for the word... leaders that are focused on God's plan for me and you. The Bible said clearly 'Michal, your prince...' Which means Michal, our leader... and since we're all believers and Christians so, Michal is the leader of the believers and the Christians... A leader sent by God for his people... Brothers and sisters, Michal is an important leader because he's a leader of the end of times. It is clearly specified that Michal will lead during a time of trouble....Not any kind of problem... the worst kind of pain - like it's said 'trouble, such as never since there was a nation.' Some painful time is coming! And it's not later than now... at the very moment that I'm speaking... Now!!"

Reverend Thompson started to read verses seven and eight of the twelfth chapter of the Book of Revelation where it's said "there was war in the heavens and Michal and his angels fought against the dragon..."...Brothers and sisters, some unimaginable things will happen... even in the heavens, the sacred home of God... Satan will try to take control an bring his miseries... The word of God specified clearly the events that will happen... Like you can see there are no mistakes, everything is precise.

The Reverend saunters while praising God by saying "the Lord is wonderful, the Lord is powerful…" Suddenly, he stopped and said: "Brothers and sisters, the Lord reveals me who personified Michal. Yes, Michael, our prince, is here this morning with us." Reverend Elijah Thompson pointed his finger on John and said "you can stand up my friend, God designated you as Michal, the leader of the end of times. "Rev. Thompson explains that John is about to take power and bring more coordination in world affairs. Although he's not giving any precision on the wars that will eventually break out, he reads some verses in the 24th chapter of the Book of Mathew where Jesus Christ predicted the conflicts that will take place.

After showing John as the leader of the end of times, for about a long hour, Rev. Thompson keeps on preaching on the "everlasting life." and the "resurrection" promised by God. The assembly is very excited by the perfect preaching performance of the Reverend. Since a lot of personalities and dignitaries are at the church, several local, national and international news cameras broadcast the event. Although John is already used to have big crowds of people staring at him, he felt timid and uncomfortable. Reverend Elijah Thompson finishes his sermon by pointing his finger and raising his arm up and saying "Jesus is on his way!".

John shakes hands with the Reverend by saying "God bless you, Elijah! You changed my life. I'll never forget that!" Rev. Elijah Thompson tells John that it's not him that changed his life but the Lord Yahweh.' did such a thing. Then the Reverend hold John's two hands together and makes a short three minutes prayer. He invites John to spend the week at his house and tells him to ask Ann to come to join them in Washington.

Ann takes the plane with all the kids even though the school year wasn't over yet. She got to Washington late in the evening with Wesley's plane. Reverend Elijah Thompson congratulates John for his beautiful family. Everything is perfect because Ann and the kids already knew the Reverend's family - and the Barlows have a lot of things in common with the Thompsons. While the two families are together, John is in the presbytery speaking divine business with the Reverend.

Reverend Elijah Thompson already had a plan for John to stand behind the rostrum of the church by next year. He thinks in all that John **seems** to be an evangelical minister who was misguided. He didn't point John's parents for the blame. The important thing is to guide John to the sanctified life of God's employee. They spend hours and hours discussing verses and praying for his guidance and forgiveness in their lives. He brings him over some church's members houses performing prayers. The Reverend starts to feel that a week wouldn't be enough.

John agrees to stay longer. And finally, John makes him understand without telling him directly that he used to rob banks. Reverend Elijah Thompson told John to spend the money efficiently and never even think about going back to steal anything - although a Christian must bring back all wrongly acquired resources. He explains to John that turning his back to the thing of this corrupt world is already a significant effort.

"John, you'll see God will give you a better life. If you pass through the same process as me, you'll feel so astonished about what's happening to you that you'll tend to think that you're crazy. A permanent surprise, that's what your life will be. You will never believe it completely. Think about it seriously, you've always lived your life quietly with your simple earthly ideas. You've probably never imagined that you would be announcing the coming of a Savior in the sky to pick up some dead and living people. Myself, I'm living a daily stupor," The Reverend is talking in a solemn tone to John.

"Of course Elijah, I already started to feel that way since the first day I got to Washington. I understand very well what you mean. That's for why I concluded that God is in my life."

"Praise Yahweh! Praise Jehovah! Our God and only one."

"You're right Reverend, our God is powerful!"

The Reverend started to sing a song along with the two other pastors who were present, to close the biblical study session. And he asked John to make the prayer:

"Powerful God of Israel, bless us all your servants, put the Holy Spirit in us to inspire us in preaching your word. Keep our children safe and obedient to your laws. Jesus, our Savior, be always with all of us. I'm asking you, my God, to give more understanding of your word and help us in believing more and more strongly in your word. Yahweh, we're all here because we're fascinated by your great qualities and your might. Please, be always with all of us your ministers - in Jesus-Christ. Amen."

"Excellent brother John! Indeed, God will answer your prayers! I can't believe it, God already started to change your life." The two other Reverends hit John's shoulder in a sign of encouragement.

After three weeks and two days in Washington D.C., John Barlow took his private Challenger airplane to his house in Town of Mount-Royal. His sojourn in Washington with his friend Reverend Elijah Thompson was unforgettable. John feels that life is so mysterious. He's lucky to know a little bit more by uniting himself with God. Knowing God is the best thing that had to happen to John in his entire existence. He's not about to forget that for a long time.

"Cheer to the Reverend - come on move your hands!"

Jessica said: "Bye! Bye! Reverend Elijah."

"God bless you all! Bye! Bye!" The Reverend really like John's kids. It took a long time before the plane starts taxiing. The two families were exchanging a lot of last-minute messages: "tell Wesley to call me! Make sure you pray more often John!" It was indeed a scene that any moviemaker would record on his camera. His experience was more exciting than taking some vacation on a southern island by degrees Celsius.

John couldn't stop watching the skies through the windows thinking that he probably won't reach the top job. In his head, there is no way for a true Christian to do anything that has to do with business, POLITICS and underworld activities. The future of a Christian down this earth is poverty, hunger, unemployment. His own life story can prove that only the disobedience to the law will help to live either decently or indecently. Everything is a matter of HARD CASH. John will understand correctly the way to deal with all these things through his Bible and his new career as a Reverend.

They say that Dong King may not do illegal things, but he does immoral things - Dong King wears his Catholic Cross and states that he's a Christian. John Barlow keeps all his stolen CASH and thinks that his conversion to Christ is still active. These questions rolled for hours in John's head, and no answer comes to his mind. And suddenly, John started to realize that he is new in the Faith and he has to take it easy.

"What's wrong with you Darling? You seem to be absorbed by something that is bothering... Don't worry... I'm there for you... hum... huh..." Ann asked gently to John.

"Nothing. Hum... Huh... Just thinking..."

"You look so worried... Tell me... I wanna to know..."

"...Hum Huh... Do you think I look like a Reverend? A man dedicated to God."

"Ah!... ah!... ah!... ah!... You're so funny, Honey! You don't have to look like a Reverend. Only God will decide if he wants you as a Reverend... Look at you... you make me laugh! Stop thinking about that okay!"

"Yes, Darling! I'll stop thinking about that," John tells Ann.

John Barlow started to think that along the years, Ann has always known how to comfort him. Sometimes he was sure that his lovely wife could read his mind. In another way, she probably knew everything the day when the police shot several bullets at him. Is she an angel or what? He doesn't know. But he's thinking in his mind that every good wife must be an angel of God. By examining himself, he started to believe that there is no such thing as a good husband. Even if all the men of this earth are not like Pepper, a violent officer, an ex-military convict, and an elite gang-member - or like him, John Barlow, a killer, a violent bank-robber and a silent, deadly gang-member, they still don't worth the hand of a bride.

The Challenger jet is about to reach the sky of Montreal. Ann is still hooked to John by a short nap in his arms. She is turning her head on him like he is a good pillow. All this brings him to think that it would be almost impossible for a man like him to become a Reverend. It's probably true that females are God's worst enemies. John seems to listen first to what Ann is telling him. Will God find a place amid them? After all, Reverend Thompson prophesied that he will become a leader, a chief of state - not a Reverend. A leader manages national resources, and a Reverend lead the Gospel.

As the plane is losing altitude to approach the landing site of the Dorval private airport, John could see an army of people waiting – as several security guards are trying to stop them from invading the track. Some ten to twenty cameras of news along with journalists waiting for the prophetic prince.

"Mr. Deputy, do you think Reverend Elijah Thompson made a false prediction about you?" A prominent news anchor from Toronto asked him.

"The future will tell - like everybody knows, I'm a great believer... And if God chose me, let it be so...," John answered as an experienced politician.

"We have information that you started to be more biblically oriented... Does that mean you're about to change your career by becoming a Reverend?" A female reporter from Montreal asked him.

"Nothing has changed in what I'm doing... I'm still the NDG riding Deputy who went to visit some friends in the U.S.A... That's all," John replied carefully.

"Mr. Deputy!... Mr. Deputy!... What... Can you...," a lot of journalists that couldn't reach John after the scrum, they were calling him to answer some other questions.

John Barlow embarked the eight doors Limousine sent by his office to pick him up to his house. His seven crew political team is following him in another car. One of John's closest advisor, Mr. William Morrow tells John that according to his information, the Prime Minister is about to resign his position. Since there are only six months left to the mandate, they will immediately call for a Leadership Race for the Party. The Liberal Party already belong to John's clan. Wesley already arranged everything with the financial supporters like the companies along with the delegates.

Prime Minister Kevinley Eaton could resign at any moment. His replacement, Mr. Peter Miflin is very weak politically. Even though the Prime Minister who is not a particularly good friend of John, can decide to pass his entire staff and contacts to Deputy Mifflin. There is no way for Mifflin to do anything useful - POLITICS is not something that goes well with him - he's an exam "passer," not someone who understands." The rule of the field is that there is no such thing as a clear political question. Nobody should try to answer clearly: you just say something for "the sake of the birds."

Mr. William Morrow informed John that Dr. Julius Robertson is in town. Actually, Mr. Robertson called two days ago and asked for John. Dr. Robertson is partly finished with his Supreme Weapon project for the Army. He did his M. Sc. and D.Sc. in subjects that are closely related to the arms project. The scholar studied in many fields such as economics. He's a genius that can excel in any academic discipline.

Dr. Robertson is looking forward to talking to John as the next top civil officer of Canada. He's well informed about all the new things that are about to be developed. The scientist is the kind of person that can keep John up to date on almost everything - even the most dangerous ones. John already knows that Dr. Robertson is a wanted man because he's working for too many people at the same time. And sadly, the Americans don't like kind of guy like Robertson even if the scholar would follow everything they say. The reason is that they don't want smart people who are not part of their nation. The name of the game is that Robertson will fall on one of the Western countries' SECRET SERVICE bullets one day. If there is no reason, they'll invent one. "Smoking" people is the primary rule of business down this earth.

John agreed to meet Robertson on a Friday at 18:30. The meeting will be at Robertson's house in Westmount. Four bodyguards will accompany John since it has been confirmed that Robertson is on a hit-list. It's way out of John's mind to don't help a Canadian to survive an assassination plan. Now he thinks that it wasn't a good idea to let the WESTSIDE-CONS down. But in reality whatever you let down won't let you down if you still have some HARD CASH in your possession.

Westley already checked which organization is about to kill Dr. Robertson. The ex-Pepper knows that most governmental organizations leave their dirty jobs to the criminal gangs. Only one nation wants Robertson dead, and three posses are in charge to do the job. We're back to square one, another war is on the way.

CHAPTER 6

The encounter with Reverend Elijah Thompson was reminiscent to John. All that he told Rev. Thompson always come to his mind at an inopportune time. It's the guilty feeling of living on the resources that he took from some other people. There's also the idea lurking in his mind that he won't have that money anymore. For now, no one could possibly take the hundreds of million dollars that he has - and surely the trillion of Pepper.

While on vacation in California, Pepper received a call from a weird individual stating his name as Mack. John told Bradford that person must be some US secret service agent and nothing else. Mack invited both of them at a governmental office in Houston. The only hint Westley was given that it's about his deceased dad.

"You mean my father is alive?"

"Not exactly that. Something more thoughtful."

"What is it, then?"

"It's about your inheritance."

"Ok, I'm coming right away."

It took him four hours. From the early morning when he talked to Mack, he took the plane with John. At around 10:30AM, he was walking on the streets of Houston, Texas. Both two friends were sitting in a cab, looking at the city's constructions through the

Buick's windows. Their conversation wasn't at all about some kind of speculation what Westley's dad left for him. The only thing in Westley is thinking about, it's that someone read his mind by telling him precisely what he's interested in. What's the warlike story of his father like the British officer, Mercer, who depicted most of the Waterloo battle before he died?

In front of the building, there were some seven soldiers gathered as a circle. In fact, it's the office of the boss of the entire USMC in the country. Pepper was thinking that his desk would be on a base or somewhere. After all, it's a government building with many high-level administrators. On the Building's board, Westley saw the name of the highest rank commander as General Frank Kellogs. Actually, the general and his command staff were waiting for him, and it's now 12:17 at noon.

"Hello, son!"

"Good morning, Sir."

"You seem to have felt the twitch of your father's death on the battlefield."

"Yeah, we've all lost one in this country."

"My condolences! We have something he left for you with your real name on it. No government is able to give you a better gift."

"What is it, general Kellogs?"

"That's the beauty of situation: only you know what's that surprise from your dad."

"You mean you will hand me something from my beloved deceased father that you the C.I.A. don't know anything about?"

"We have a lot of respect for our members' memory."

The general made a sign with his fingers telling all his command staff to leave the room. John went outside the office also. Westley sat down as General Kellogs is unveiling a huge box. There were many papers in his hands as he pulled out a couple of envelopes and told John to take a look.

"You have absolutely no obligation whatsoever to tell us what your father left in those letters."

"I wasn't thinking about telling you anyway."

"Believe me, that's fine by me. It's intimate, and we want you to keep all the secrecy with you as your father surely wished."

"I'm grateful to you, Sir."

"You're welcome, son. I knew Shepherd very well. Don't hesitate to contact me for anything you want."

CHAPTER 7

Every day, John would meet close to ten people according to his plan to build an excellent contact network to support his future government. Although he's still a timid man, most of the people he met like him a lot like the next top boss of the country. The future MP always tries his best to explain his agenda with the most critical issues. The big problem for John is that there is no logic at all in what he's doing because of the ultimate goal is to get the power. Especially in a democracy, nothing seems to be in anyone's control. He keeps pocketing his supports from the most powerful and the wealthiest.

Most of the people who are with John are assured of his strategic capabilities to push nobody around in carrying his administrative tasks. John encourages everybody in what they're doing - even the badest people. He told the Metropolitan Toronto Police chief that by being evil with the criminals, he will encourage them to get worst.

The only threat that John faces is that he often proposes a solution that is sometimes contrary to the advice of professionals in the field. He's careful enough to consult these experts before saying anything that would damage his relations with them. John tries to always give the impression that if he did something wrong, it wasn't on purpose.

However, a small incident happened with CEO Kate Bentham who told him that a new technology caused the layoff of sixty-seven employees in their plants. John mistakenly asked her about the lay-off terms. Since Mrs. Bentham is a vulgar person. She told him:

"what lay-off term! We didn't need them anymore, we sent them home." She's with John because of her colleagues.

He manages to forget Mrs. Bentham and keep going. John promises the homeless people that as soon as he gets to power, he will make a special program for them.

"You will give each of us a house!" an old man asked him.

"Yes. That could be part of the plan," John replied to the man. "Don't worry, we have enough money to do that."

"Why don't give us the money now. We need the cash while we're alive not at our death," another man told John.

"Just wait until I get there. I will become the next Prime Minister anyway. A lot of people support the changes that I propose."

"Yeah! Yeah! Just another one with his promises. Go to hell!" a group mumbled.

John is sure now that the destituteof the society seems to be far from him. He thinks that he lived like a rich for too long and he is not able to understand them. The deputy candidate is serious about what should be done to ease their pain and to overcome their difficulties. Definitely, his message can't get thru, although he will win the elections. It's clear that these poor people have no influence on him. He can forget about them just like his predecessors.

He met with Robertson like planned. They drink some Jack Daniels while talking together. Robertson told him:

"I surely don't want to live to see what's going to happen in this world. My passion for science is killing me because it's the main reason why I invent weapons."

"Maybe you should stop that," John replied to him.

"It's too late. Me and you, we won't exist anymore after the use of the arms that I just made."

"What is it exactly, Dr.? Can you be more straightforward?"

"At the time we're talking, many belligerent countries are equipped with the updated version of the canons that I built with Gerald. Not only that, my new special rocket is there too along with the aircraft and some other state of the art explosives. NATO just lost its military supremacy five months ago, and these countries want revenge. The U.S.A. and Canada are facing their first serious military threat."

"How can you talk like that? Don't you have a security level?"

"You seem to forget that you re a Deputy, also the next probable Prime Minister....Kind of things like that can't be a secret to you."

"What do you see for repairing the situation?"

"Nothing. Absolutely nothing. We will all blow out!"

"When would that be?" John asked.

John doesn't know that Dr. Robertson is in an impossible situation. His real name is Salaam Abu Jeloun. He's from the little village of Maaloula in Syria. Since the beginning of his career as an engineer, the Arab governments mandate him to develop weapons and to send the archetypes to their organizations. The Supreme Weapon is already mounted, and some tests were already made. Although he's on a hit-list, they still didn't clearly identify his association with the Arab organizations. Robertson was ready now to tell John the most crucial information - a terrifying one, indeed: "...Like... At the time we're talking the threat we use to pose to these countries is on us also. Some long-range missiles with nuclear warheads are ready to be fired at us and our allies. The enemy has the counter-measures against our missiles..."

"What about the projects that you're working on?"

"They're outstanding but inefficient concerning readiness....And John, one of the reasons I'm telling you all that is because Prime Minister Eaton is about to resign because he doesn't want to handle these things... And forget Miflin to take his place... in a situation like that." Robertson is cautious to don't let John even think the possibility that he's the traitor that is reinforcing the enemy's army. He's well considered by the American and Canadian military establishment. They suspected him because they're trying to find a spy. But as an experienced politician, John is entirely sure that Robertson is not on their side.

"If all you just said is true... why this silence?" John asked him.

"It's probably like the "calm before the storm.""

"Where did you get all this information? It's bizarre..."

"You can call Stanley Bannatyne at Los Alamos, he will tell you the exact same thing. Not a word more, not a word less."

We could hear the calming noises of a device. It's the cellular telephone of John that's ringing.

"Hello! It's William."

"Hello, William! How you doing?"

"Fine. John, Syrian Forces and Jordan Forces just cross Israeli border. Prime Minister Eaton will announce his resignation. I already call the

Liberal Party - by emergency measures, you've been declared as the party leader. We can already form the new government."

"Not so fast. Wait! Wait! What did Mifflin say... And according to the constitution... Article 92... 94... can you please verify the legality of all this..."

"You're already the Prime Minister."

"That fast!...I'm not sure of that..."

The noises of the Canadian Army Griffon helicopters over Dr. Robertson's house is evident. A squadron of five choppers along with airplanes could be heard all over the Town of Westmount. The Chief-commander of the Canadian Armed Forces, General Andrew Lexington is on board a Crown Victoria with two officers of his command staff. The car stops right in front of the 516 Victoria. Then General Lexington says:

"You're Mr. Deputy John Barlow!"

"That's correct General!"

"I was informed that you will form the new Liberal government to lead Canada in the next twenty-four hours....We're in a critical situation, Sir... Our troupes must be ready to move ASAP. Let's hope that we'll be able to stop our territory from invasion... It won't be easy!"

"It's a terrible situation! I heard about it. We must react quickly. What do you know about the extent of the forces that are being used?"

"The Israelis have already moved a lot of forces... We're talking about 150 thousand troops... It's what they call their Third Army, which integrates Air force, Armored, Artillery and long-range missiles. The Arabs defenses are enormous... The Americans informed us that the Arabs mean business this time..."

"Do the necessary for now! And give me seven hours after I get to Ottawa to form my government."

"The main problem is that we don't know what the enemy has in mind. The hypothesis is that they will try to invade the entire Israeli territory before they get to us. It would be essential to know the stand of the nuclear powers that are not part of NATO - Russia, China, India, Pakistan, South-Africa, and the Eastern-European countries."

"Okay! No Problem! Don't forget... in seven hours from now." The General and John look at their watches and say together: "It's 20:30 you at 03:39!"

As Prime Minister John Barlow embarks in one of the Griffons Parked in the middle of Sherbrooke Blvd corner Victoria, General Lexington salutes him. He is surrounded by soldiers in combat gears, handling Thompson Canadian riffles are commonly known as C7 along with BROWNING pistols at their hips.

John is heading to Ottawa where he will arrive in thirty minutes. In following John's command to do 'the necessary,' General Lexington gives the authorization to deploy 50 thousand troops all over Canada to train the population in emergency drills like NBC, Air-bombardment, first-aid and all other measures.

While travelling in the Griffon, John is calling everywhere to pick the ministers of his last-minute government. Thirty-two civilians and seven militaries will meet him in Ottawa to form the government. He already talked to most of NATO members, and they seem to want him as the leader because he proposes them to meet in a British base near London to determine a general strategy.

Conceding the situation that the Arab armies are into Israeli territory, General Yacoub Mohiacovah takes the decision to send the 250 000 troops of Israeli First-Army deep into Egyptian soil to establish a robust backup position for the forces inside Israel. If the strategy succeeds in the next five days, Israel will be able to tell if it can contain the Arab armies. They don't know if the Air force will be able to hold against the new fighters with the CONVAIR engines developed by Dr. Robertson. Two thousand of these new fighters that can comfortably fly at seven times the speed of sound are in active duty in the Arab armies.

The Army moved the Barlow's belongings to Sussex Drive. John's government is already discussing the ways to deal with the risk of a nuclear attack or ground invasion.

It's 01:00 o'clock, John didn't sleep at all just like the members of the government. The Americans already sent five-hundred F-16 to Israel's army along with one-hundred extra pilots. US Navy fires several missiles on Arab military targets unsuccessfully. None of the arms hit their goals - they've been intercepted with a lot of precision.

The US Navy researchers are working around the clock to find a way to counter the effective Arab air-defense system.

John is in the living room of his office conversing about the situation. William is there, of course. Three other advisors also: Robert De Normanville, Gen. Fred McDonald and Col. Bryan Edward. The advisors make John think that he can handle this crisis. Col. Bryan Edward is confident: "The other nuclear powers outside NATO will adopt a neutral position." They all think that countries like Russia won't take part in this war.

"We can certainly forget the idea of winning or destroying the Arab armies. A good possibility for us would be to bring the conflict to a dead-end and force a cease-fire," Gen. McDonald said with conviction.

Col. Edward replies that the enemy already erases the nuclear threat with its state of the art air defense system. "If they want to conquer the land, our armies can force a dead-end."

"The Arabs want some kind of revenge, they will kill and destroy everything in their way to punish the opponent," Robert De Normanville suggested with a pessimistic tone.

A messenger holding several fax sheets advances and hands them to William. The documents were sent By Russia, China and India to express their decision to don't be part of this war or any other wars. John starts to feel a little bit more confident in his advisors.

From the Parliament office, we suddenly hear a typical strange sound of a chopper. It's the Canadian Army Griffons helicopters that just arrive at Parliament Hill. General Lexington's get out of the helicopter parks on the Parliament landing deck and says to his aide:

"The Prime Minister knows that we are here?"

"He's about to... The sergeant is going to..."

It's 02:45 and John didn't expect Lexington yet.

"You mean he's already here asking for me," John told William.

General Lexington is walking thru the corridors on his way to John's office. As a Prime Minister, you feel worried when the commander of the armed forces comes to see you surprisingly. The militaries always know something nobody was aware of, especially in a time like we're serious threats are pending over the country.

"Sir! Sir! Sir! The situation is deteriorating. Our forces must move ASAP!"

Lexington was talking loud while some other people were listening. William closed the door of the office as the defense Minister joins them. Everybody look and listen carefully to General Lexington as he's throwing his information all over the place.

"The American Join Chief of Staff thinks that all the Israeli forces deployed will be encircled in the next weeks or months. It's been confirmed that no matter what they do, they'll be fighting in retreat. We must help TSAHAL now or forget about them. The Arabs will burn them like charcoal if we don't move at the present moment!"

"I have a meeting with all NATO members in England, in less than twenty-four hours to determine a general strategy."

"Sir, if we don't forget about that meeting, for now, they'll be toasted. It is imperative that we deploy our forces in the region no later than ASAP. Our people are ready - just waiting for approval."

"Okay! Call NATO contacts in England, France, and tell them that we have a joint deployment in the Next hours."

General Lexington takes his cellular telephone and call to give the signal: "get everybody rushing to the Middle-East!"

The order of Lexington makes a domino effect among Nato members. A clear account of the troops and equipment deployed would give something like 100 TRILLION DOLLARS. Also, nobody believes the announcement of neutrality made by Russia, China, and India. The Arabs are probably bargaining to see how much

CASH these countries want. It's just a question of time, they're indeed working their way to total extinction. John thinks that maybe Robertson is right after all: "we'll all blow out!"

It's been confirmed that Wesley doesn't want to be part of all that political thing. Especially that bloody nonsense war which just started, although it clearly indicated that we're not in the case of an imperialistic war.

"Robertson is a strange guy", Wesley tells John. "I mean the guy knows everybody all over the place but he just do his little researches and that's it. Why is that?"

"You mean he must be an important piece in all what's going on all over the world."

"Affirmative! I don't trust him. He's the kind of guy who would work for two enemies."

"There's one good thing about him though, he has the solution for any problem."

"Actually, Robertson told me that the war is part of an impossible situation."

"He's lying. There's nothing impossible for guys like him. He's Jesus-Christ in person... Some people heard him talk about race and other things like that..."

"Robertson is a WHITE MAN. And he's one of the world's top scientist. What does he have to worry about?"

"He's probably just an image of somebody we call Robertson. The real person is maybe completely different."

"I want to know who he is... You hear me, Wesley! Find who he really is..."

"Hum... Hum... I'll find out! Don't worry you. Any of the world secrets always hide behind words like CASH, WHITE MAN, GUNS... Robertson is somewhere in there..."

John still ignores his powers - the leaders of NATO are waiting after him to stop the Arab troops. He's able to lead the entire world, but he doesn't know that. The Supreme Weapon or any engineering idea that Robertson may have are useless in front of John's leadership. Robertson knows that, but he didn't have time to tell it to John because of the Griffons and General Lexington.

According to the military reports from the front, the Arab armies are winning. The moral is very good. They did an excellent demonstration of brutal force. American military strategists have estimated that within the next eight months, the Arab armies will be able to claim a complete victory.

However, if they are to contain the Great Attack planned by NATO, the western countries could be invaded. During the entire month of the beginning of the war, the U.S., England, and France were mostly observing the actions. If the show of force is equal, maybe the nuclear threat could force a peace accord. After all, it's Israel that is being attacked, not the U.S. or England. As a long time ally, the U.S. must retaliate against the attacker.

John is going to Washington next week for a critical meeting with the main NATO members to discuss the nuclear issue. It looks like nobody is rushing to go to that conference. There won't be any theory down there. Everything will be real. The fear of probably all the humans on the planet will become a reality.

From his office on Sussex Drive, John can see the people who are passing by waving their hands at him. They're more encouraged to shake their hands because of the conflict that is going on. And they know that the coming of enemy troops in Canada is not an illusion or some kind of speculation.

"Mr. Barlow! Will the Arabs come all the way to Canada? I heard that they have a lot of armies," a young lady who was passing by the window said.

"No! No! It's only in the Middle-East! Not here."

This is a clear Demonstration of the absolute refusal for a Chief of State to let the public life at the rhythm of their fears. And since the Middle-East is well known in the media, the news about the Arab armies attack couldn't be or wasn't adequately controlled.

There are more and more people close to the Prime Minister's residence, and placards saying: DON'T SHOOT THE MINUTEMANS IF YOU CAN'T BLOCK THEM!

Some protesters would yell: IT'S OUR TURN TO BE ATTACKED!

As the hours are passing, the number of protesters reaches about twenty-five hundred. The security didn't intervene because the crowd wasn't menacing. John's Press Secretary decided to install a microphone along with some speakers. The idea was to enable John to speak and reassured the protesters that no severe military action has been taken and the Canadian territory is not at risk.

"I've been an MP from the NDG riding in Montreal for seven years, and there's nothing that I cherish the most than the military security of our great country - which you and your children!..." John said with as much sensitivity as he could.

There are always people to trap those seductive leaders as they try to hide their fears behind nice words.

"We didn't say that you don't want to protect us! There are missiles that are able to come all the way to Canada in a matter of minutes! Even if you want to - if you can't..."

"This is not the truth! Ladies and gentlemen, that is not correct! We are not threatened at such an extent. If you wish to, the government will distribute a brief in the next hours to inform you of the exact situation for Canada."

John talks to the protesters without any plan. All the people surrounding him are happy about the performance. It's just like whatever the risk of a nuclear attack, which is ugly, the goal is always to make a great show. Actually, John is a real political beast because he's an evil man who is still trying his best to be nice.

Saturday morning, we're June the eleventh, John is on the phone with Lexington. The General and the American military chiefs think that Israel will probably consider the idea of shooting a nuclear missile.

"Of course we'll be able to convince them to don't even think yet of using such a weapon. These countries are in a panic, and we know it's tempting...," General Lexington said with the risky attitude of hiding his fears. John is already talking to his Defense Minister of the possibility to replace Lexington. The militaries, even the Americans are mumbling that the man is very experienced, but he's not a warrior. Beyond the high-ranked officers, some people laughed when they heard that he was in charge of the entire Canadian Armed Forces.

John starts to feel the real stress of leading a whole country as several subjects are mixing up in his mind. That big box of NATO, the de facto replacement of General Lexington. He also needs to know what to do at every step of this war. John will pay anything to know if Lexington has something to do with the transfer of the Israeli Prime Minister's telephone call to Washington.

He is startled to watch television like any other citizen. The effect of following the news that he makes himself. Around 18:15PM that day, he listened with William and Robert, the news report of Elliot Shift From Israel: "Early, this morning, Lebanese and Syrian forces battle their way thru the security zone between Israel and Lebanon to reach the city of Hebron. Although the Arab armies step into the ancient city, some brutal scenes of combat are still going on in this particular area. It's quite sure, this house-by-house battle could last for weeks and even months. Altogether, this great war that just started between the two nations is not about to stop. Both sides have already put a lot of forces into the conflict. We're talking about Israel's First, Third and Fourth Army. And on the Arab side, there are twenty-two divisions, 650 000 men, 2500 tanks and about the same quantity of other vital types of equipment. Rumors are already running that Arab forces will triple soon to carry a very destructive attack that supposedly will annihilate the entire Israeli Army. But western support is growing day after day to help Israel in its effort to vanquish the enemy - an enemy that attacks first by crossing the borders of a sovereign country illegally.

Eliot Shift, CTV news, Hebron, Israel."

After the report, John walked out of the TV room and went to his office. He is thinking about the possibility of missing the meeting in Washington because the situation would be too critical. Actually, when the Israeli Prime Minister called in Ottawa to speak to John, he wanted to tell the Canadian leader that he was thinking seriously about shooting a long-range nuclear missile, not only to try the enemy's defense but to win by other means. Before that, a particular unit had already the task to take control of all the launching sites. Since the beginning of the conflict, the only aim of the U.S. was to claim the complete control of the situation. Also, the fact that the Arabs have the military capability to hit American cities exacerbate the fears in Washington. They needed to have the ultimate command of the war.

It looks like everything will fall on the right timing because of the C.I.A. has a perfect message for the NATO countries. General Lexington communicates the news to John:

"The Iraqis will give the last push to the Arab attack. General Victor Hussein is being appointed to burn, kill and destroy as completely as possible everything on his way. For that, his cousin Saddam gave him 1 400 thousand men, eight thousand tanks, 45 hundred planes, and all the artillery that he would need. Take my word John, or Sir, General Victor is not anybody, there will be nothing left in his way..."

The Arab armies are sure of one thing in sending General Victor Hussein, they will dominate the Middle-East.

"We better send all the forces that we can... if we want to stop them!" John said without any technical military reference.

"Also, they'll probably start to shoot the "big pencils" to bring the drama at its peak."

"General! it's the last orders! You have the entire control of our forces until further notice. Except for the missiles."

While General Lexington is informing John, a lot of changes happened. The Arabs just launched two long-range nuclear missiles to Omaha, Nebraska. The "pig pens" are being detected eighteen seconds after they left their launcher. The U.S. Air force 2AD-INM (Intercontinental Nuclear Missile) unit is activating the interception procedure:

"ECHO-U.S.-2AD-INM just visualize INM in progression to target".

The first sergeant who's in charge of guarding the unidentified object. The 2AD-INM is a five-man crew. Two persons are in charge of gathering all the information on the missile. Their job can't last more than nine minutes. After that, the two other men will each on their turn look for the plutonium or the nuclear heads, depending on the brand and model of the atomic content and the country that made the missile.

Now, the communication between those five men has fifteen messages and answers. The interception process is still active:

"ECHO-U.S.-2AD-INM, keep watching INM to target, INM speed MACH-15, Three ionic engines."

"ECHO-U.S.-2AD-INM, keep watching INM to target, INM is heading Nebraska."

"DELTA-U.S.-2AD-INM, INM on CHARLIE'S control."

"CHARLIE-U.S.-2AD-INM, INM charge location.

"CHARLIE-U.S.-2AD-INM, INM charge is three, two empty."

"BRAVO-U.S.-2AD-INM, INM time is twelve minutes."

"BRAVO-U.S.-2AD-INM, INM ready for unloading."

"BRAVO-U.S.-2AD-INM, INM is unloaded - ready for destruction."

"ALPHA-U.S-2AD-INM, INM charge destruction is in process."

"ALPHA-U.S.-2AD-INM, INM-1, INM-2 are all destroyed."

"ALPHA-U.S.-2Ad-INM, INM's interception mission is complete."

After those long nineteen minutes, the U.S. Air force commander told the Joint Chief of Staff Commander to inform the U.S. President that the interception was a success.

The President ordered an immediate retaliation of three U.S. Trident on Iraqi, Libyan, and Jordanian soil. One of the three missiles will be shot from a mobile launcher in Europe.

For all the missiles in Canada and the U.S.A., there are probably twenty-two hundred launch-rooms, along with the same number of interception-rooms. When the two rockets were shot from the U.S. to the Middle-East, John could see everything on a screen in Ottawa. It's a big show to see all the coordination and the military fashion in which all that is done.

"US-NM-f-27, NM-612 (Nuclear Missile) is hot."

"BRAVO-US-NM-F-27, NM-612 will leave By President."

At this point, the President is giving the launch-code to unlock the missile from the launch site. The President is speaking from wherever he may be.

"President-Lancer(code name) 12-6-7-34-D-CER, complete approval."

"DELTA-US-NM-F-27, NM-612, repeating combination: 12-6-7-34-D-CER."

"ALPHA-US-NM-F-27, NM-612 missile unlock, pushing the shooting button. NM-612 is in the air and will be guided automatically to target."

From there, the launch-room will follow the missile until it hits the target. Now the launch-room knows if the enemy activates an interception process. In this case, the Arabs did, and their interception-system is faster and more accurate.

The three missiles were intercepted and destroyed successfully. The American military establishment is in panic. The western army technology supremacy is apparently over. The battle is dramatically equal, or it looks like nobody has an advantage.

Now, it's obvious, we are in the case of an all-out war and the U.S.A. move their alert to a dangerous step; DEATHCON-3-B means that fifty percent of the country's forces are in use. The U.S. Air force itself is handling 3 500 F-16, and they're shooting short-range missile like 5.56mm M-16's bullets. The US never thought that the war would go so far. From the alert of DEATHCON-3-B, the president called an urgent meeting with their Joint-Chief Of Staff commander, General Brand "Crow" Knolton. It has never been a questioned of massive troop deployment because the primary strategy of the U.S.A. has always been to promote peace throughout the world. Also, the Pentagon Foreign Affairs department is very surprised by this sudden war. Most of the army's top officers didn't see anything substantial in that missile firing exchange. It's also a soldierly attitude to don't be stressed by anything, even when real incoming nuclear missiles are heading the national territory.

Strangely, the high-rank officers seem to know so many dirty secrets of a government that nothing ever really worry them. The world affairs have become something that they can predict its development in advance. It wouldn't be too crazy to say that wars don't just start without being calculated. Before the 2nd World War, the Greek billionaire, Onassis, was always talking like he knew such event was about to take place. We would tend to think that this international tycoon caused that last high scale world conflict for his own business interests. Then we learned by after that it was the Rothschild's who orchestrated the 2nd World War by reinforcing

Germany and Hitler to be able to confront the communist Russia. Inevitably, some very wrong people lead the world for the past centuries. And, on the opposite of John Barlow, they didn't steal CASH in such a blatant manner. They're all doing the same thing over and over every day, which is to fool people and selling them goods and services at some exorbitant prices.

Before the meeting, the president met with the State Secretary to have a good idea about that warfare situation. Like in all military environment, the officers of the Joint Chief of Staff have their papers and their numbers ready to give a precise report to the supreme commander according to the constitution of the U.S.A.

"Apart from helping Israel to counter the enemy, there is absolutely nothing to worry about. We are as strong as them. The situation is that they reach a certain level of force and they're experimenting it. Mr. President, the eight officers who are here with me, have all our First Reaction strategy to attack or to defend in their hands. Believe me, the Arab's armies are not aware that the US still has the power to annihilate them completely. I suggest that we stay calm even though they already shot two missiles on our territory. We are the strongest, and we should impose peace in this world," General Knolton said to the President.

"General, I find it strange that you're minimizing the fact that the the enemy shot long-range missiles on US soil," the President replied.

"The main strategic idea behind the launch of the two nuclear missiles is to get us nervous for nothing. Mr. President, we have a renown scientist that is developing a weapon for us while spying for them. Our secret services informed us that they think they have military superiority. Let's put it this way, the day one of their bomber or missile will reach our territory successfully, we will order a massive attack."

"It might be too late. But, you mean there is no way for one of their missiles to damage anything here."

"Absolutely not, Sir. And, Mr. President, the Russians are preparing an attack that neither the Prime Minister and the head of their army agree on. Some very experienced Russian military advisors think that there is no guaranteed victory and it's complete nonsense to involve so many forces blindly. So, if we hear about a Russian commando on our territory, we'll send the 82nd and some other Canadian troops to give them some practice before killing them."

"General, you seem to be in control of the situation. I count on you. However, I want you to inform me of any significant development."

The militaries are leaving the conference room. A very bizarre man gets in with some other special advisors to the President. The weird man name is A. Cromwell.

"You should be cautious Mr. President. This is a prophetic war that can surprise a lot of people," Cromwell said.

"What would you suggest in such a case?"

"It's very complicated. Myself, I don't think I can handle this. But I do know Rev. Elijah Thompson, and he can help us."

"Bring him in, and I'll talk to him. What can I tell you..." Mr. Cromwell is calling Rev. Elijah Thompson on the phone. He's telling the Rev. to come to the Pentagon right away.

Apparently, no tradition have lost their flavors. There is nothing more real in the context of modern warfare situation. In the past centuries, people had to go in the tranches to live the war and get to be astonished by the glory of confrontation, courage, and bravery. Today, the well-sharpened mediatic instruments give all that bewilderment without any real presence on the battlefield. It's like Shakespeare himself wrote the screenplays for the television newsrooms from his tomb. The exquisite footages of all the aspects of the war, the politicians in their high legislatures everywhere in the world, the protesters, the battle scenes, the families of the soldiers, the mass destruction weapons, the UN offices in New York. Everything is live and entertaining. The spectators are the actors on the sets.

The phenomenon of the watchers who became more skilled than the actual people that are performing the thing. John Barlow is the ultimate product of such a fact. The PM read so many books that he got to a point where he's the teacher of the writers of the books that he learned. In the same order of idea, most of the sports fans can play with the professionals that they are deifying. The servants took the places of the Gods. undeniably, there is only one way for any God to keep its followers obedient. It's tocultivate ignorance. Light destroys all power systems or slavery as it brings equality. Everybody can do anything.

Some people took a position in a particular discipline a long time ago, and they discover some secrets that they never explained. For years, lies like prophecies are methodically followed by everybody and many great minds such as Nostradamus. Today, John Barlow will prove that there is nothing complicate and he has the answer that always fits. Now, do people know that anything they say is a prediction? Meaning a word said is an actual thing ready to come. A. Cromwell and Rev. Elijah Thompson are brilliant, but they mysteriously ignore something so simple that our ancestors have used very often. It's John's turn to prove the reality of the past millenniums.

From its congregation office located at five minutes from the Pentagon, Rev Thompson took his personal car for such a prestigious invitation. He already knew that it's not a routine meeting. Since the day John called Elijah from his office in Montreal, he kept in mind that anything mentioning the name of the PM is not only scary and troubling but more importantly grandiose and an occasion of great revelations. It's about to be true.

Rev. Elijah Thompson enters the President's conference room. The President shakes his hand and welcomes him.

"I've been told that this war is prophetic. What do you know about that?" the President asks Elijah.

"Yes, indeed, it's a prophetic war. There is only one person in this entire world that can tell you everything with more precision. It's Mr. John Barlow, the Prime Minister of Canada.

In all what's happening in that war at that particular moment, there's only one man who has the best position: it's General Lexington. The Canadian commander knows that most NATO superpowers are very uncomfortable when air force and navy technologies are useless. They use the infantry, but they never count on the infantry like some kind of a backbone. Lexington knows all that and contrary to his fellow American officers, he trusts the infantry and it probably only one on this earth that can use it efficiently. And, that makes a long time since Intelligence had an idea about the Arab armies air-defense technology advance. The high-ranked officers of NATO are talking about Lexington's infantry experience to win the war. It's now something real.

The Canadian general spent weeks evaluating and watching the improvement of the 1.1 million troops of the Canadian Army. When observing the army's training, he's looking for precision. General Lexington traveled to the U.S., England, France, and Italy and did the same thing. He wants to feel comfortable in using the infantry with surgical precision. A lot of people that are important in NATO's hierarchy believe Lexington would be profitable when the infantry is really needed. At this point of the war, something is bright, navy and air force are not as effective as they use to be. The missiles are being intercepted at a rate of ninety-five percent; the most technologically advanced planes like F-22, F-116, RAFFALE, etc., weren't that effective because of the Chinese NANJING radar. For decades, air support like missiles and aircraft were the central part of the most powerful armies of the world. With modern warfare, the infantry lost the priority that it used to have in the ancient Rome, eighteenth-century Europe or the Napoleonian army. Now, the INFANTRY took back that priority because of the lack of effectiveness of the air support devices.

The war is falling on the shoulders of the infantry and its tools like artillery, rocket launchers and all the mechanized types of equipment. General Lexington understands that. He could guess that it is his war now or if we prefer, it's his time to shine. For years, Lexington had been studying the infantry technics of the German WEHRMACHT officers and France's L'École de Guerre. In other words, the Canadian General holds some infantry secrets that none of the world army leaders know. The hobby of studying infantry history is about to pay off. Princess Patricia's Canadian Light Infantry officer is indeed pleased, even in such a scary and dangerous warfare situation.

Now, for about two weeks, he walked around the Infantry Messes in the country, and he rings the bells for his warriors like the feast before the fight. Everybody was drunk and couldn't wish a better situation than that one. Again the war has become an exclusive ground troops business, and the General is theoretically, for now, the Supreme Commander.

There is also the fact that since the beginning of the war, British, French and American SECRET SERVICES issued a HIGHLY CLASSIFIED report where it's stated that Russia and China might or will probably fight on the Arab side. Those two countries have the most capable infantry soldiers in the world. Indeed, NATO commanders will call for the best ground forces troops as possible. In such a case Lexington will be crowned as the King of NATO.

In any war, as small as it would be, some information about the enemy always remained unknown. The US is aware that the Arabs have a powerful military capability. Can they attack American territory directly? NATO intelligence didn't find out yet about an Arab's Pearl Harbor. But, when the Arab leaders saw their advantage in the Middle East, they're thinking of an attack in North America.

It's September the 2nd, the members of the US air force unit in Florida receive the message of an enemy squadron who escaped NATO fighters and keep going right into American territory. Several air-defense missiles automatically took the sky. General Knolton calls the president as three bomber squadrons left to carry a general offensive.

"Sir, the three bombers left as a normal procedure. We can always call them back."

"Call them back immediately. Do not carry any automatic military attack... I repeat, stop all our forces from everywhere no-matter-what."

The conflictual situation is degenerating, and there seems to be no alternate solution than to fight back and cause the death of more people. After his prophetic discussion with Elijah and Cromwell, the US president feels that it is imperative to take the possible measures to stop that nonsense war. Since right now, the hope is on John Barlow. Obviously, there is no time to lose. He must make it as fast as possible from Washington, D.C. to Ottawa, Canada. The US Air force Hornet can travel faster than 1.5 sound barriers. The president is in the fighting jet in the direction of Ottawa. He's speaking to John, and he's telling him that he might know something that he's not even aware of. His personal ability to stop the strong start of a third world war.

"Listen to me, John. What do you know about the Bible's prophecies?"

"You should talk to Rev. Thompson. He's the one that predicted me as Michael, the leader of the End of Times."

"You know more than that. Now, don't forget, it has to do with the war that is happening."

Less than one hour later, the fighter carrying the President is landing as Prime Minister John Barlow is waiting. Both, Rev. Thompson, Cromwell, and the president are walking together before embarking in a big limousine.

"Concentrate yourself like you were a prophet of God. You know everything, and you are the only chance to save a large number of people from dying," the President told him.

"I told you I don't know anything. And, I still don't know anything."

This last answer of John breaks the President trust in his prophetic abilities. He called Rev. Elijah on the side to confirm his assumptions about the PM. There are many doubts.

"Are you sure that John knows what to do? He said he doesn't know anything."

"He knows... The reason why John knows is that there is no man on earth who would deny being God's prophet if he's being told so..."

"You mean nobody would refuse such a title. Why is that? Anyway, we don't have much time."

It's like a giant complicated puzzle falls at the PM quarters at parliament. Everybody is looking where they can possibly find the solution. One problem is never enough because three men just check in and they're walking toward William. The men are telling William that they must talk to the Prime Minister. Actually, the men are angels because they just appeared at Parliament like a magical dove. William is walking with the men to go see John. One of the men is telling John that he needs some business connection for his company's new products in Asia. So he wants the Prime Minister to call some Asian leaders in Thailand, Cambodge, and China. John shakes their hands and assures them that everything will be done for the success of their business.

The three men are leaving the office very fast. Reverend Thompson and the President come back. John says to them that three strange men just 'came to see him and they left. Thompson doesn't really know what to say, but he's trying to remember a quotation of the Tibetan leader.

"The Dalai-Lama said that he's "like the reflexion of the moon on water and anybody who looks at him, that person is looking at himself." I guess that these three men were angels. I believe that God sent them to help John," Reverend Thompson mumbled.

"You mean by seeing them, I will become an angel of God?."

"Indeed, I would be a way to communicate in this instance the power of God by letting you three angels that kind of force and knowledge."

"I know! I know everything about the prophecies. Fundamentally, there is no truth, Jesus predicted the wars like he would create them. If we want to stop the war, we simply need to predict peace and create the peace."

"Do you understand something in what he's saying, Reverend?"

"Hum... He means that our Lord Jesus didn't need to predict any wars or sufferings and all that... Yeah! Yeah! Keep going, John..."

"In other to predict better times, we'll simply take a piece of paper and write precisely what we want to happen."

For the first time in his entire life, John Barlow brought something utterly new to mankind of this planet. He's trying to present the idea that the commonly known placebo effect in medicine has biblical and therefore spiritual applications. The purpose of a suitable medication is as good as the medication itself. So Jesus would have made the mathematical mistake of saying things that he doesn't wish to happen. In other words, a man who feels good in a bad situation is a man who he's destroying such condition. The magical properties of the spirit of men which are based on his will to only imagine and see what he wishes.

In following the idea of predicting the end of the war as a way to stop it, John and his advisors along with William are writing a document they call:

"The Troops Withdrawal and Peace Agreement." They describe in detail how they would like the war to cease. The President read the treaty and agree to it. Even if they don't have any proof of the results, they're all happy and thinking that it will work.

The US President is spending an entire day in Ottawa. He's thinking about going a little bit more east to go fishing in the province of Quebec. But the principle remains that a man of duty like a head of State can't entertain himself while his country is at war. He's preparing himself to leave for Washington. Before taking place on board Airforce-1, the President is confident that it's just a question of time before the war stops for everybody's advantage. But for now, some major troop movements and many bellicose men are actualizing more violently, because of the modern warfare technologies, the historical battles of two enemies.

CHAPTER 8

The Middle-East is hosting the most vicious battle scenes in its longtime conflictual history. The Arab countries like Lebanon, Syria, Jordan, Irak, Saudi Arabia formed and half circle deadly front imagined by the sadistic mind of General Victor Hussein. One hundred percent of the Israeli war capabilities are involved in the war. Except for the highly secret strategy of NATO to hide since 1985 an army of 1 500 000 men and the equivalent equipment around Israel essential cities. This secret army formed five harsh lines of defense.

For all wars, the number of troops and the equipment is only a small part of a winning combination. The brain, the character and the qualities of the strategists are more critical. It's like two excellent and skilled boxers confronting each other. In the past centuries, the stake was high because of the resources, lands, and gold. Today, there is more nonsense than anything else. But on the Arab side, General Ahmed Victor Hussein is the head behind everything. His opponent, General Yacoub Mohiacovah, presents all the characteristics of a genius military leader, although he doesn't have the will and the motivation to carry wars. Whatever the two chiefs combat files may contain, they both look alike as they are ready to fight.

When looking closely at the Middle-East's war situation, the Israeli army is in lousy position regardless of the intelligence of its supreme commander. General Hussein's ruthless army wants to maintain the initial advance. The Israeli forces must create stronger positions as it will enlarge the battlefield. Since the enemy knows the army's capability and numbers, they will surely look for the rest of the military that will go to Egypt. General Mohiacovah to build up as the 4th will join them for some kind of a bridge. In such a situation, the Arab armies would do something right by not trying to push them out too fast. If they wait, the supplies can go low and enable them to have a better advantage for the victory.

A critical problem is crushing the Arab armies. General Hussein is a brilliant man but too illogical. He has the psychological talent to conduct men to carry the aggressive actions on a warfare theatre. Now, the war has become something too severe for most of the officers and many troops. The reason is that the conflict is personal to General Hussein than a national cause. Every time, the commander has shown to his men that he lives for wars as he fines it joyous. The honor code of serving his country as a defense against any intruding force died a long time ago under the leadership of the General. Although it doesn't look like it, every army and country need a model that it will impose on the outside world. As a brilliant and dangerous man, General Hussein will show them the ideological goal.

No one really understands the reason for this particular war between the two nations. Back in history, the creator of the Koran, Mohamed, opposes the commonly known divine stories of the Bible. The Israelis who are the main followers of the Bible don't accept the idea that God would have sent a second book and another great and last prophet, Mohamed. Not only that, most of the Arab nations and people use to be the Israeli's enemies. Several Arab lands are the real soil of significant biblical events. Necessarily, these territories were conquered from the past Israeli's armies. And, spiritually these servants of God thru the Koran are not considered as God's believers. It's a simple hypothesis which is base on the prophecies of the Bible. For the Israelis, God keeps his promises. And, Mohamed and the Koran is only a tactic to counter them spiritually. The logic for the Israeli people is that the Koran would be right just if God is not sacred and the most truthful of all what is known to mankind.

Arabs and Israelis give the impression that they're struggling against each other for God's favor. When observing these two nations in their religious practices, it's like there is nothing else that matters most than praying. Since Judaism is commonly accepted as being established before Islam, it wouldn't be a mistake to consider the fact that the Arabs tried to be in front of the Israelis by praying more than five times a day. The problem remains that the Koran accepts all the biblical books, the Old Testament only. The New Testament is declined just because Jesus isn't considered as what they call a begotten son of God - according to the Islamic view, God can't have a son like us human being. Somewhere, Mohamed and Jesus would represent the divine mysteries and all that is unclear spiritually to mankind.

Now, an important question that is well answered in the Bible, but it cannot easily be adapted to modern times. God said in the Psalms that the evildoers will be cut off and Noah proved it by warning the people of his time to follow God's commandments. Nobody was obedient, they all perished. It's bizarre that when it comes to biblical writings, most people like to speculate. The Israeli nation paid a lot for the defilement of God's temple and the disobedience of the divine prescriptions. In the Bible, the prophets seem to have announced the same thing in different ways and words. The prophecy in the book of Daniel reported the coming of the leader of the end of times by the name of Michal. In that same era, the deaths will be raised, and the judgement will come to reward the ones that deserve such a thing. There wouldn't be a mistake to consider that prophecy to be able to cover all the other predictions of the other books about the coming of a Deliverer. Indeed, according to the Bible and allthat has been considered as the truth for quite sometimes, the goal of Islam is either evil, unclear, false or utterly malignant. In such a case, the Muslims are part of the evil forces that the people of God must counter. That's for why the Middle-East can't be a land of peace. Anybody that   comes to understand very well the concepts of Satan and God will admit that the two can't agree. And, as a simple fact, a long time ago, the Egyptians built their kingdom by turning the Israelis into their slave worker. Like it wasn't enough, they wanted that to be eternal, but God intervened to stop that from happening.

Indeed, it's a weird coincidence that today, in the same land where the Israeli people took over a long time ago against an all-powerful Egyptian army, they will try to do almost the same thing. Close to the borders of Egypt and Israel, General Mohiacovah is standing in a Merkava tank looking at his troops' movements with goggles. He breeds and feels all the events that happened on that sacred land. As a matter-of-fact, it's only now that he thinks that he knows this land is holy. He stated that he feels a giant thing like a strong force is surrounding him. He's absolutely sure that it's the God of the heavens and the earth.

"What are you talking about Yacoub?" a Major asked him.

"God is there, believe me."

"We're soldiers, and we're being fooled by the money people. They pay and train us to be disciplined and do everything they want, just like dogs."

"I'm telling you, Eloyim is with us like he was with Moses."

"I think that you're getting insane, Sir... The time has come, I'll ask them three brigades to charge on the east side and stop after fifty kilometers like you told me."

For General Hussein, Mohamed leads over everything. He also accepts the idea that the Koran is close to the Bible. Apart from that, his job and duty are to kill, enemy or not. He has a leading position in the army, and he has ordered that he will obey at all time - the perfectly trained dog. It is to be remembered that Hussein was born in Lebanon where as a kid he visited an armory and became fascinated by the arms profession. Before entering the academy, he showed his talent and strength to kill men. Nobody can confront the officer physically. He's also very skilled intellectually. There is no attachment of any kind in such a man. The historical events happened just like anything else.

In maintaining their advance deep into Israeli territory, the sections in charge for reconnaissance reported the Israeli's troop movements in the direction of Egypt. The tactic of the Israeli army is to show that they are going to Egypt when they're already there. Now, what the men of General Hussein saw it is the fourth army's race to connect with the first to form an all-powerful bond that will push the Arab armies back in their territory. People have always asked themselves where do the officers stay when an all-out warlike is ongoing. The respected courage and bravery of the army's leaders make that the troops never worry about such a thing. It's not accurate to say "be an officer if you want to stay alive."

The first and fourth Israeli army form an angle point that is ready and on his way to push back the enemy as far as possible. Apparently, the nineteenth and twentieth-century war leaders, like Pétain, Foch, Ludendorff, Bismarck, Paulus, Voroshilov, Joukov, Rommel, and many others, would have been shocked that we're still carrying some giant stupid army manoeuvres, just like they use to do. Now, as a part of their general and ruthless offensive, the Israelis are systematically destroying the bunkers and all the other enemy constructions with missiles. When preparing himself to leave his battlefield headquarter, General Hussein's bunker exploded with a gigantic blast of PETN missile explosive head. He died at the instant. The news of his death halted the army and stopped the motivation of the men.

Since the war is continuing, the Arab armies are progressing very fast on the positions of the First and Fourth Israeli army. The scenes are sadistic, and they're using the modern version of mustard gas. General Mohiacovah and some other officers are outside watching the performance of their troops closely. It's like anything else; the memory of a man is limited. If he's too preoccupied with some other things, he must remind himself of the most essential item for a complete success. Most of the battlefield gases are odorless, either somebody thought about such stuff and protect himself or utterly forget it for another drama. The officers surrounding General Mohiacovah and himself are all dead as their body started to decompose by the gas.

Several hours after the dramatic events of the deaths of the two war leaders, the Israeli Prime Minister and the Arab Coalition Leader arrange a meeting on the Golan Heights. The reason for the conference is that the Israelis succeeded in pushing the enemy as they want to catch their breath to conquer. And the Arabs wish to reorganize their army from a leadership crisis. Plus both countries know that the west is arranging some peace meeting where they must look good by showing their will to sign a peace treaty. The Middle-East is obviously the center of mankind destiny where a theological truth will decide the wrongs from the rights. The wrongdoers will suffer and die.

Since the day John gave the entire command of the Canadian Forces except for the two thousand and more missiles to Lexington, he spent his time organizing the rescue and emergency services for the population. In a way, the general is taking care of the war with the Defense Department and John are arranging safety facilities.

"Just build underground... everywhere... Make sure everybody knows the basic cures... and you know..."

John was speaking with the coordinator of an emergency organization that he just created. Actually, it became a national organization. Then General Lexington calls him on the phone.

"The two missiles that were intercepted... Does that mean they will, or they can all be destroyed before they damage the target... I mean the cities..."

John was anxious to have some technical information about the enemy's defenses.

"That's exact Sir! Interception efficiency is being estimated as one hundred percent. Sir! All the air support devices are now useless. Everybody is talking about ground forces...," Lexington felt a little bit comfortable.

"You mean the infantry can carry nuclear heads to enemy territory?"

"We can always do that if we're loosing... or before..."

While John is talking on the phone with Lexington, William brings two letters. One is from the Chinese government, and the other is from Russia. The notes are war declarations. Since yesterday, Russian commandos have already started reconnaissance mission to prepare an invasion by Alaska. The US President orders the Defense Secretary to suspend all war support to Israel until further notice. That means until they push back the Russians.

The Russians shoot twelve SS-25 modern version missiles with explosive charges to some petroleum production site and some essential manufacturing facilities in Canada and the U.S. All the rockets were intercepted and destroyed. NATO retaliates from its launching locations in England and the U.S. with sixteen POLARIS, TRIDENT and MINUTE-MAN. Two missiles hit the chemical and nuclear production facilities in thecity of Kiev by igniting a massive blaze. The Russian kept their offensive by ordering KGB agents to conduct some sabotage actions against petroleum and nuclear production buildings in Canada and theUnited States. The province of Quebec Gentilly II facility and he East-end Montreal petroleum production plant were the targets of the destructions. The installations took on fire, and they were damaged at eighty percent.

Now that a third world war has been started, a killing contest between the humans has begun leaving on its back nothing than desolation, deprivation, sorrow, and tears to all parents and relatives of the warriors. It is not a spectacular or beautiful scene. It is a scene of horror and ugliness. Conceding the fact that we still distribute medals and honors to the most distinguished soldiers that find the way and the heart to skillfully give death to their fellow human beings. Is there anyone at fault? Anyway, that war and all the other ones prove that we're not following the same policy and procedures even though we leave on the same planet and we're biologically identical. The war is happening, and the eyes that are looking will tell everybody how it was - to see and hear agonizing and dead people. All the countries of NATO give the last war orders to their respective army. Everybody knows that once nuclear particles come from an explosion, the communication devices like radios, television, and telephone are out of use. Obviously, it's quite a miracle that no major nuclear explosion from any missile didn't happen yet. Most of the military commanders are in complete surprise.

The fact that several treaties of non-proliferation of nuclear arms were signed didn't matter at all because the top-secret government documents revealed that the nuclear arsenal of NATO was never decreased. Some old Saturn and Titan rocket was destroyed. The primary state of the art atomic weapons remains in use in ground and mobile launchers, or in the submarines. Since 1993, NATO knew the effectiveness or the air-defense systems technology that has been developed in the world. The researchers never found something to completely solve the problem. Also, the fact that the air-defense systems are so effective brought a guarantee that the treaties couldn't reach. If the nuclear head doesn't explode in the air at a certain altitude, it's capabilities will be diminished because the main idea is to have the radioactive particles to travel with the wind and to cover more territory. This war is getting all the armed forces of the world very scared. To tell the truth, there is only fear and nothing else. In the last meeting of Nato commanders, here is the word of American General Brand "Crow" Knolton:

"Until further notice, Canadian General Andrew Lexington will be the commander of all the armies on the ground. His main task is to stop the Russians and their allies from invading Canada and the U.S. along with preventing the Arabs from taking the Israeli's country. We know that our air and Naval forces are presently useless and the same thing goes for the enemy. Gentlemen! The War is on the ground only! And General Lexington is our expert and our hope! We're lucky because I know what I'm talking about. God will help us! Gentlemen, we will win."

"At least we don't have to worry about anything in Europe. It's certainly not today that the Russians will go down and take France, Germany or England," a general said like a joke.

Surrendering the fact many countries of Nato are technically at war, there still no significant troop movement here in Canada and the U.S. The military security reports didn't mention anything suspicious at the borders. It's August the 1st. Since July the 29th, Russians elite commandos are carrying reconnaissance patrol to prepare the way for a massive advance party of a million men among the best of their army. Canadian and American forces didn't see anything yet. There are five hundred Red Army special forces soldiers prospecting the regions of Yukon and Alaska. They're at one thousand miles inside Canadian and American territory.

Three Russian submarines are dumping military equipment under the water for the five hundred men who already landed. Many divers are carrying the materials to the dry land as some other members of the commando are mounting them. There are artillery pieces, anti-tank, different ammunition, and all other crucial infantry apparatuses. It's dawn now, and the parts of equipment are ready to be used. The commando can carry its task. A Sergent-Major, the second in command reports to Colonel Vatievski, the commander in chief of the commando. It's clear that this quite unusually big prospecting battle group is operational. Colonel Vatievski is going thru the combat drills with an extreme ferociousness.

The verification is affirmative because the group responded very well and showed the ability to provide sufficient firepower that can counter any numerous army. Now, a Russian General is coming out of the water while being accompanied by seven soldiers. He's in charge for the entire Russian invasion force. The soldiers are walking with the General in a guarding formation. They are getting close to the commando's camp as the chief, Colonel Vatievski is called to meet the General. The commando's leader is now approaching the General as he salutes.

"At ease! At ease everybody!" the General yelled to the men. He's now walking with the Colonel. They're talking.

"Colonel Vatievsky, if the Canadians know that we are here, you and your men will be abandoned," the General specified.

"You don't have to worry about us. We can take care of ourselves. Failing is not a habit among us," the Colonel responded.

"You know how stupid you've been to decide to come here. Vatievski, you want to tell me that you don't know that this is a cover-up."

"I don't know what you're talking about. Just bring your men in when I'll give you the signal."

Colonel Vatievski salutes the General as he's leaving with the soldiers that are with him. They put their underwater combination and go deep into the sea.

The problem between Colonel Vatievsky and the General is related to the fact that elite troops never mix well with ordinary army soldiers. Since right now it's a question of numbers, the general is trying to take advantage of the situation by putting some pressure on the special forces commander. And Vatievsky is one of the finest of Russia's high-rank officers. The General is challenging him a little bit.

Even before the 1st World War, a long time after the U.S.A. emerged from its crisis of the Civil War, everything has turned out to be a game. On the West part of the world, life is fun, and it's an atmosphere of joy. Science and technology are progressing very fast. America is a center of attraction for many citizens of other countries. Some artists from Europe are dreaming of a career in Hollywood, New York, or just anywhere south in North America. In a way, the stories of the Far West have strengthened Americans. And, the game of war, as dramatic as it could be doesn't matter at all. It's more important now to make money and have a good life. That's where the business started to be the high interest. There is no issue, no cause, no honor, only money is at stake. Did the psychologists, psychiatrist, and psychanalysts caught or noted down that significant concern of human beings as a scientific fact? Maybe not, maybe yes. They became very interested in the Hierarchy of Needs of Abraham Maslow. Anyway, the convinced and stern people are being fooled all the time because of all this.

Now, for some reason, the idea of a war between the US and Russia has been well-cultivated. Why? Nobody knows. It's a fact, a long time ago, the US made their biggest business deal with Russia by selling them three hundred thousand firearms. The Americans didn't appreciate the Bolshevik revolution and the expansion of communism throughout the world. The possible confrontation between the two giant nations was and remained an entertainment just like the highly publicized boxing championships. Which means Russians and Americans have always been good friends.

In a very nice restaurant near Boston, Ma, an American top military advisor is meeting the ambassador of Russia. The two men would see each other at least three times a year. It's a standard, non-professional encounter. That's probably where these people reveal their secrets. The citizens would feel more confident if they would know what is being discussed in such an occasion.

"It's like the world has never changed. We make some weak people believe in a fictitious war. The goal is to show that there is something serious happening," the American advisor said.

"Yes! Yes! You must be right. Our two countries will stay in business forever. But, Vatievski is serious... he's not joking at all."

"Who is Vatievski? Another Rambo who doesn't know how to have fun."

"The best officer in Russia today. He needs to grow up and stop shooting riffle for nothing. Vatievski is leading the commando we send in Alaska to prepare a false invasion."

"He volunteered for that position... I guess... What does he have in his mind?"

"We'll let your two countries make a coffin for him. At the army headquarter, they said that they will abandon him if your troops see his commando."

"We heard that the PM of Canada is responsible for paying some people to kill General Hussein and some other leaders to stop the war. These guys must be pleased right now; they were paid seven thousand billion dollars…"

It's like everything was prepared in advance. Two well dressed gorgeous women approached the two officials' table as they keep on speaking and laughing ruefully. The females took place and sit down as they show their will to be part of the conversation.

"You don't always come here… I mean…"

"We've always been here… all the time."

"I like the food… the salad is delicious…"

"The simple thing of meeting nice people. I mean it's fun…"

"Of course… right…"

After the missile attack on the facilities in the town of Kiev, the Russian military strategists had a crucial meeting which would decide their probable pull-out from the war. They thought that some more powerful type of weapon could be used against them. The Russian Prime Minister feels that if the result of the war should be equal or not in the total favor of Russia, he will ask the President to call back the troops. Actually, the authorities in Russia are seriously thinking about the destructive power of a nuclear, biological and chemical weapon. The fears of the Prime Minister about the possible total annihilation of Russia are real. When the two missiles felt on Kiev, the situation exacerbated. It is correct to say that the government already decided to stop its involvement in the war after the offensive on the nuclear facilities.

The defense system to counter the missiles is remarkable. But for some, reasons the militaries couldn't explain the events in Kiev. Most of the generals knew that they already lost their chance to demonstrate that Russia could carry a very active war against the west. Some officers are thinking about assassinating the Prime Minister to continue the warfare. The army doesn't really care about winning or losing even if they have a dreadful start.

"The Prime Minister doesn't trust us because of Kiev. What can we do? Russia has the force and the strength to beat America! I'm not going to let a stupid civilian weaken Great Russia," a General who is the senior military advisor said.

"We can always kill him. There is no problem Sir! Like the Americans say the Prime Minister is "cooked." He will die skillfully like a coward dumb," a high-rank officer told the general.

Contrary to western military command meeting, Russian officers never report all the opinions to the government. So the officer openly suggested the killing of the Prime Minister. And they all agree to the murder idea. The commanders were necessarily offended by the fear of losing that is troubling the Prime Minister. A separate group affiliated to the official KGB would carry the assassination plot. The strategy of the killers is to give an overdose of sedative to bring the man to think that he's sick. And his personal doctor will conclude his death. For the murderers, even if the Prime Minister would still be alive for a while, he will be so sick that he won't be able to assume hisgovernmental position. The officers are so sure of themselves that they already consider him as a dead.

Like bad luck, the wind is not blowing in the right direction for the militaries. A group of campers came across a section of the Russian commando in a little town in Alaska. Some of them speak English very well, and they don't wear the former Russian combat uniform.

"Hi! Hi! You are beautiful! You like soldiers - I can tell. You girls seem so excited," a corporal said.

"Of course, we like soldiers. You guys are so courageous. I mean I wouldn't carry all those pieces of equipment."

The five men had two ANTI-TANKS, three machine-guns and their personal weapons with all the necessary ammunition. They also had some other equipment like explosive, a mini-radar, etc. Most of the commando's members were trained for those kinds of situation. Although the conversation with the three female campers could have to take a better turn, the Soldiers felt too busy doing their essential work.

Some other soldiers of the commando were being seen, and the Canadian Army was informed of their presence. It took exactly one hour to identify the troops as Russian special forces. The American 82nd Airborne is being rushed to the region between Alaska and Yukon. Seven hours later, Canadian 1st and 2nd Battalion of the Royal-22nd along with some Navy Seals provided the reinforcement. Then an entire NATO army formed by the Canadians and the Americans encircled the whole small and strong Russian commando.

Colonel Vatievsky doesn't know precisely what Moscow wants him to do. The Prime Minister would definitely ask the commando to stop their mission immediately. Now that the coasts are under high surveillance, they already forgot the option of returning to Russia. The only idea in Vatievsky's mind in the present circumstances is to fight their way out by blending in the population with their civilian clothes and try to disguise their equipment.

From the report presented by the Prime Minister, the President of Russia already gave orders to stop all the military actions that were previously approved. Since the generals were in a meeting, the Prime Minister called the central command directly and ask an immediate an end to the operations.

"Sir, I need the command of the General in chief! He's the only one that can give such a command," the officer in charge told the Prime Minister.

"Forget about the General in chief! We need you to stop all the military operations, not later than right now!" The Prime Minister yelled at the officer.

"Okay, Sir. What about Vatievsky's commando? The Canadians and the Americans already encircled them. And we can't get them back to Russia through the submarines," the officer is very disturbed.

"Abandon the commando. The Canadians and the Americans were informed six days ago that Russia will stop all military operations against their armies," there was no hesitation on the Prime Minister's face.

In the region between Alaska and the Yukon, a radio operator for the Russian commando is trying to contact theRussian forces at home unsuccessfully. They called Moscow over and over without any answer. The colonel waited one hour while he couldn't reach his commanders in Russia. Colonel Vatievski is telling his Sergeants that Moscow evidently decided to abandon them. The sergeants tell Vatievski that NATO troops are looking for them in the area. Many soldiers that are in charge of patrolling confirmed the presence of some ten thousand soldiers close to their positions.

"Since we are abandoned, they don't care about us and our mission. We must escape. Take the escape routes with most of the men as a small portion of us will cover you," the Colonel said in Russian.

"Okay. We must be fast, the closer to us now," the Sergeant-Major mumbled.

"Move now! Let's go! Let's go!"

He flips coins to pick fifty men that will stay with him to fight while the four hundred and fifty other men will pass through the lines of the Americans and Canadians troops. Nato soldiers are now at a reasonable distance. The planes are already attacking. As Vatievsky is asked to put down his weapons because he supposedly disobeyed to Moscow's orders. The colonel orders his men to open fire on NATO soldiers. Several planes drop bombs on thecommando's tranches. In return, the commando guns down twenty planes. More than forty Nato soldiers are already dead. The Commando is very mobile and agile. Tanks, soldiers, and planes are going down at a higher rate. There are explosions everywhere.

MARINES Colonel Lane Perry is speaking with his commander at the army headquarters.

"Sir! I personally request that you send my Marines no later than now.! It's a whole gaggle here! These people don't know they're left from their right. Even if we're a lot here, I assess the situation as hopeless!" Perry said to the General who leads all the US Marines Corps.

"Watch your language Colonel, you were sent on this battlefield as a leader to motivate the soldiers and win. I expect you to do what we ordered you and nothing else. There are no Marines which will be sent to you."

"Sir! I repeat, there are good soldiers out here, but for some reason, we are in a bad position. Don't forget Sir, I'm not used with the 82nd Unit and these Canadians! Send the Marines!"

"That's all you got Perry! You have to make it with them!"

The Colonel is forced to close the radio as the raging noise of machine-guns, anti-tank, artillery, and riffles seem to be coming close. NATO body count is still rising, and they also lost many planes. The battle is getting more ferocious.

NATO commander, Colonel Lane Perry, the former MARINES African-American officer took the blame for the mistake of his superiors that sent too many forces against the commando.

Some American Blackhawks choppers are fighting their way to the battlefield with General Lexington on board to secretly stop the damage. Before arriving on this large combat zone, Lexington already knows what to do. The General is stepping down the Blackhawk helicopter as Colonel Perry is running toward him. After being saluted by Perry, he told the Colonel that it was a big mistake to put a big army against an out-numbered commando. Perry knew that, but he was ordered to charge the commando, not to give his opinions.

Lexington is taking seven hundred and fifty men beyond the Navy Seals, Canadian 1st and 2nd battalion of the Royal-22nd Regiment and he told them to go and get that commando.

"They're five hundred men! I want them all," Lexington told Colonel Perry.

The Canadian general knows that he's fighting a lost cause for the reason that Vatievsky has several options available to him and his men. Lexington can't really control the movements of the commando. Actually, the Russian elite force stole two trucks and three APCs along with some Canadian and American combat uniforms. Vatievsky and his men got wheels, and they're getting out of the bushes to take the Alaskan military autoroute.

Colonel Vatievsky lost three men: Corporal Alex Groushnov, Sergeant Boukine Parsolov and Sergeant Vastei Bisniev. The colonel ordered his men to carry the body of the soldiers with them.

Since the beginning of his communication problems with his commanders in Russia, Vatievsky has one idea is to get to the

Russian Embassy in Ottawa. He Knows that it's a very dangerous and risky idea, even if he succeeds. The Russian Embassy is well guarded by policemen. According to international law, he should avoid contacts with civilian forces. The four hundred and fifty men that left a long time ago contact Vatievsky to tell him that they got all the necessary equipment like a bus and cars to move around as they want to. But the problem remains that they're four hundred and ninety-seven men plus the Colonel, which means that they can't go in at the same time. So they thought of separating themselves into several groups to go to different Embassies' in Mexico and the U.S.

When the first group arrives in Ottawa, the soldiers basically drove on the fences and make some kind of a barricade with their vehicles. The authorities didn't know that they were from the commando. As cops were rushing toward them, they run inside the yard and state that they're Russians. They were lucky because the Russian government didn't have any evil intention for them. They were abandoned because there was no way to recuperate them.

The second group would go to the U.S., and the third and last group with Colonel Vatievsky is set to arrive in Mexico some four hours after all the two groups would be safe in their respective Embassy. Of course, as soon as they come, they communicate with the Colonel.

Lexington's men found all the weapons that the Russian commando left behind. John personally called the General to tell him that he doesn't need to search for the commando anymore because they fought their way to different Russian embassies. And excellent news about the Middle-East will be announced. Apparently, the Arab armies are ready to accept $15 THOUSAND BILLION to pull out and to give a part of Lebanon to the PalPalestinians who will receive for themselves only $7 000 BILLION. John smiles when telling that it was one of his new political tactics to stop wars with CASH.

In Asia, the Chinese were cautious in accepting to support Russia. Since the beginning, China never wanted to start conquering with the other countries. Without sending any official message to Ottawa, the Chinese followed the Russians when they announced that they won't pursue the war.

On Monday, September the 18th, NATO countries met the representants of China, Russia, Israel, Palestine, Egypt, Syria, Iraq, and all the other Arab countries to sign a treaty of non-military aggression and the complete destruction of all mass destruction weapons. The entire world could breathe again without the fear of war. Actually, a vast American organization started to travel the world to make sure all the countries respect the peace treaty.

Before the end of his mandate as Prime Minister of Canada, John and General Lexington became excellent friends. They had dinner at Sussex Drive along with Wesley and their families. Robertson flee to Syria before Wesley had the time to find his real identity. Lexington likes Wesley a lot - of course, they speak about infantry sometimes.

"I think his name is Vatievsky. How can a commando rob itself from the American 82nd? And the Navy Seal... plus MARINES Colonel Lane Perry. Jesus-Christ helped them or what?" Wesley tells the General.

"Yes. It was a very good commando. Don't forget those troupes were abandoned by their superiors. Certainly, they became more alert when they knew that they were purposely left there to die. Somebody told them something they weren't supposed to know," Lexington said to Wesley.

"Also, their tactic of presenting themselves as a battle group when they were, in reality, a giant patrolling force that will avoid confronting an enemy face to face."

"Be careful, we're talking about a group of special soldiers that already built powerful defensive positions to counter any kind of attacks."

"Charging them right away wasn't the solution... more preparation, maybe."

John couldn't ear anymore about those discussions about violence. A lot of people surrounding the Canadian Prime Minister, including General Lexington felt that it was time for the countries to stop arming themselves. The Canadian government defense department had a new role to start influencing the other countries of the world to completely dismantle their armies.

Deep inside his mind, John knows that the world will be what we want it to be. He wants to put the weapons away because of a simple reason of priority. In fact, something very mysterious that he can't really define is dominating all his world disarmament program. John thinks that there is no logical reason for any conflict other than stupidity. In his mind, he's thinking that mankind has been fighting disastrously since the dawn of time for absolutely nothing.

The dreams and the peaceful ideas of John will probably erase the fact that he's a warrior. And there is nothing more common to warriors than battles. Also, since there are plenty of causes or things that need to be done, John will keep being in action. There is probably no answer to the question which is to know why do some people oppose themselves to logic things. Is it the pure ignorance of it? John's opponents are still numerous and robust.

CHAPTER 9

We know that he spoke several times to Dr. Robertson about Welfare Economics. He read or study extensively the same subject. Naturally, John developed some kind of a fascination for this particular field. As a prominent politician living in a modern social oligarchic world, he's about to influence the present economic system of Canada and the globe profoundly. The oligarchs of the planet are not about to give up on him. John is thinking of breaking the policy of the world to give access to privileges to everybody. While aiming at efficiency, he's not aware that his implementation ideas for Welfare Economics have a long time ago the theoretical and fictitious hypothesis stages. In the effort of clarifying the subject, some good ideas came up with some operational implementation plans in real life. Also, John is writing a lot at the same time he was reading. He already has some kind of a Bible like a step-by-step manual to change the actual liberal economic system for a welfare one.

John is finishing the last pages of the document explaining how to implement Welfare Economics. He's writing the last words. Now, he selects the "print" icon on his computer. The text is currently being print as Ann is opening the door of the office.

"Wow! Darling, I didn't know that you were a writer. Can I read it? John looks very nervous as Ann takes the fifth page of the document where it's written in big letters: MAXIMUM ALLOWANCES.

"Yeah. You can take a look. Although it might look confusing to you," John answered.

"Johnny baby didn't Pepper told you to stop these political subjects. Look at me! These things won't bring you nothing good. You think you're some kind of Lenin... for Christ sake!"

"Stop it okay! I'm allowed to write my ideas even if some people don't like them. Anyway, this document will stay in the safe. You feel more comfortable now!"

"I know what kind of beast you are. You'll put the manuscript in the safe while it's already in your head. And, you'll keep index notes of it with you... I know you, John Barlow!"

The document is printed in full as John lets Ann takes care of putting it in the safe. John is looking at the window with his arms crossed as he gives a serious look to Ann who is gathering all the sheets. At the same time, John's document is being copied in full by a hacker. We're at the office of the most prominent investment firm in Manhattan. The venture firm belongs to a man who is the director of an organization that regroups the most essential investors on the globe. When we read a thesis like the one that John wrote, we come to understand how economics works all over the planet. There are probably only three or fewer countries that are entirely independent economically. In such a situation, they are obliged to exchange their goods and services. Not only that, several decades ago, most of the countries of the world agreed to the text of the Humans Rights Declarations. Morally, a state must pay assistance to the supposedly poorest ones. It's been a quite long time ago since we've discretely approved the idea that the resources of the world are everyone's. But for some reason, the first capitalists found the way to invent a speculation system which is the stocks market. The only or the primary goal behind that is the protection and the continuous growth of the wealth of a particular group of people.

Now, mankind has been mistakenly following some myths for too long. In fact, when somebody seems to be questioning Christian ideas, they try to punish such an individual. It is clear that there is no reasonable basis to validate a statement whether it is true or false. Not only that, who will stand up and say that Jesus Christ made many incorrect assumptions? There is an efficient tool represented by science to inquire and to establish the truth. According to science, John found out that economics is elementary: many people on the planet need to live comfortably, and economics must provide the way to make that happen.

Nobody really knows that life is more a question of the group than anything else. The issue was already raised about how the startling British writer William Shakespeare came to be well known and successful. Even better, we don't have any idea about the way to get to the head of some prominent organizations. The truth is that high positions and power itself are base on wealth. And there is nothing darker than the way people like John Barlow gets to slide themselves at the head of an all-powerful machine like the federal government of a North-American country Some years ago, the builders of the power structures of society knew that. Most of us have always thought that the official violence groups were created for the protection of the national territory. It has never been our ancestors' idea to preserve whatsoever. In each area of the countries of the world, official gangs were organized to take a better part of the resources. And with time, like today, the groups of power came to be more internationally oriented. The members are well picked and screened. For worse, they always have a right hand on an extremely professional non-executive institution like the army. In such a situation, it's like each citizen is on death-row.

People tend to think that to do anything, they just need to fill out a form like the institutions promised them. Indeed, for anything ordinary, it always works, and the promises are being delivered. When it comes to important things like climbing to the PM position where John puts himself, you need to be a monster that kills your fellow human beings. Eliminating or "smoking" people is a code that sends the message to be accepted in the power positions. Now, in the entire world, it is impossible to count the number of individuals who are completely unconscious of where they are and what they're doing. Indeed, some people are living their dream. Just like Richard Nixon was dreaming instead of skillfully "waste" anything that would be potentially harmful for his presidential position. Of course, Nixon was too much of a peaceful cheater. The powerful and wealthy right-wing groups ate the US President raw - an uncooked meal which wasn't that delicious but certainly digestible.

During his trips with Pepper, John met a quite smart and efficient US Senator. The influential American congressman knows probably more things about the power than anybody on earth. It's the meeting that took place at a mansion in the State of New York. When John and Pepper met the Senator, it is well to say that they felt some kind of a big appetite for power. Also, the two good friends thought at the time, they would never place themselves against such a leader, like the Senator. Even with his thorough military experience, Pepper would have barely thought to be the opponent of this representative of government from the State of North Carolina.

It is undoubtedly a mystery why some solid boxers never confront each other. They never had the occasion would be a just answer. Since every fighter has the will, it's acceptable to say that destiny didn't want. On the contrary to his predecessors, like Allende, Lenin, Guevara, all the other "just-cause" militants, John is on the way to a battle of pure force with an uncommon enemy. John's opponents and strong opposition rely on the fact that in history, the real social struggle had always been announced but cancelled every time. Stalin, the supposed man made of iron, was scheduled to confront our western countries and its miserable economic system that is strangling all the so-called Third-world countries of the planet. It is incredibly smart to think that a big misunderstanding happened and the fight never took place. The misapprehension is based on the 2nd World war that the capitalists invented to methodically break the course of winning socialism. In some extent, it is good to say that the Vietnam conflict did the exact same thing: a significant number of people were protesting for social chan and common sense, the establishment created a war for the citizens to put their attention somewhere else than into a faulty economic system.

Now, it's Thursday, and John is scheduled to address himself about the war at the next parliamentary session. The idea of presenting his document on Welfare Economics is not in mind. He's relaxing in the living room of the Sussex Drive residence thinking about performing his tasks as Prime Minister more efficiently. But there comes a time when papers and lectures are not a man's job anymore. The moment has come to hold the gun and waste the idiots. John probably never thought that in the entire world, some individuals should be dead. And nobody would be able to convince him of such a thing. He even believes that the unfortunate events which happened in his life were some kind of bad experience in a little kid's curriculum on his way to becoming a responsible adult.

The US senator from North Carolina called John's office, and the people there were smart enough to tell him that he will call back. He talked to Pepper before.

"What do you think man?" John asked Pepper.

"I would say that it doesn't look good at all. It will be a goddamn war."

"Why? He was very close to us since the beginning," John mumbled.

"Wake-up man! You think these people are your friends. It's a powerful man! If you didn't do the right thing, you would fall. Nobody will fall with you!"

"So, we're in trouble."

"You goddamn right!"

Although John didn't say anything against Pepper's ideas, he doesn't approve any of them. And, it's important to note his confidence likewould be taking poison and thinks that it won't make him die. The PM believes that he will always live and be happy for eternity with Ann whether Jesus-Christ returns or not - and every human on this earth will be saved.

He called back the US senator.

"Mr. Senator, how are you?" John asked with respect and introversion.

"Yes. I'm fine, thanks. You will come back to Parliament very soon?"

"Certainly. I will report all about the war. In fact, I have some kind of a state of the art project about a new economic system that I won't present for now."

"I want to ask you to don't present that economic system project whatever its virtues may be. Our friends are heartbroken about that project of yours."

"Mr. Senator, it's not for anybody to be unhappy or not. Let me suggest that efficiency should prevail in any situation."

"Whatever it may be, your document is presently damaging many important investments."

"So you don't think that we should plan to give a better living standard to each and every person on this planet. Or if you prefer, if people can't think the best, we should consider the best for them."

"John, I got nothing to do scholarly discussions. You've been holding the gun with Pepper for us, and nothing has changed. You can shoot by forgetting all about your goddamn document and your socialistic ideas. And that's it! Nothing else!"

"Fine Mr. Senator! Fine!"

The senator is now talking to the people from the investment office. Everybody is convinced that John looks strong and lethal. They won't be able to keep their extreme wealth as a privilege over a large crowd of people. Although two or more individuals agreed to work with John, the team spirit of the investors' group beat them. A group always have a terrible effect on any person. They conclude their meeting by deciding to destroy everything that holds John's project and himself. A long time ago, when Fanengen called to give the blast at Pepper's weapon hideout, every important police and military organization of the world knew about it. Since the official violence groups never question the validity of orders instead of carrying them, some people close to the senator called a special task force of the US Army to hit Parliament Hill and Sussex Drive with PM John Barlow. The secret is so big that nobody will know who called the army. Now, some loaded men, psychologically trained to do what they're told, no matter who talked to they are on their way to execute the most morally uncouth mission: crushing their own head office.

Again, the commander is Remy "Hyena" Thunders. Colonel Thunders was twenty-one at the end of Vietnam. He packed the upper left side of his uniform with ribbons in the Eastern, African and Latin America countries. It was never a question of winning or losing. He basically swept all living organisms of the places with bullets and tells himself that if somebody survives, he should die. The assumption is wrong because Pepper is alive just like him.

According to colonel Thunders, it doesn't matter which country you're from: if you do good work, you'll work for him. The British have proved that opinion with their Gurka regiment formed of only Nepalese men. And, the French Foreign Legion have men from all the countries of the world. Since the small group of people that controls the CASH have internationalized everything, the men in arms were secretly separated from their national flag. It's certainly bizarre. The army has no flag since a quite long time ago, and several modern warfares happened. The truth is that only money was at stake. Nobody is to blame for anything because the rule says that you'll have what you ask for and many people weren't smart enough to demand the best for everybody apart from themselves. Colonel Thunders have a sick mind: he's unhappy if he fails to do what they told him. He called twenty of his partners in Canada who happened to have visited Ottawa at least once in their entire life because they are part of the regular forces of the Canadian Army. The tradition of the official violence groups with their professional steel method is so well to craft that the men who were contacted by Thunders are ready to perform the task even though it's against their own people in the country where they live.

In such an occasion, nobody travels in uniform. The meeting point is in American territory - nobody knows why. At a particular time known as Saturday, August the third 1997, time sixteen hundred, sixty-three men extremely skilled in the art or science of giving death will assault the very legislative head of their own country. When we're observing the disastrous moments of other dictatorship of the world, the militaries from the western countries know perfectly that in the course of carrying their orders, they can, and they will do worse. Actually, the army never has an opinion about anything if it hasn't been asked or ordered so. And, people tend to always associate this institution to its original task of carrying wars, but in reality, the militaries can perform any work - in fact, all the civilian ones.

The task force is operating methodically by dividing their plan into three stages. For the first, it's a standard debriefing like a game plan where each person and group are assigned to their respective role. It goes as such:

"Its mission as usual gentlemen, nothing new! We're going to assault a place and come back. Each of you already knows what to do. Let me test the truth of what I just said", Thunders shows a hard face. For now, the colonel is calling the teams and individual by their task name. It's a drill.

"Bravo-tiger 1!" Colonel Thunders yelled. The man responsible for this particular team answers: "as soon as I heard the order to attack, I keep on shooting and blowing up everything I see for the next fifteen minutes, then I hurry up to regroup with the others and leave."

"Right on! Right on! Perfect!" the colonel said with confidence. It's impossible to think of a better plan because Thunders is the only one who knows that the primary goal is to kill PM John Barlow. Looking at the militaries, before an operation, it's normal to think of a professional dancing group or orchestra rehearsing before a presentation.

Everything is precise just like when the Israeli task force assault the terrorists who hijacked a plane in an African country. The mission was so well executed that only the leading officer died. While colonel thunders are on his way to Ottawa with his wolfs, Canadian intelligence has already recorded a part of the conversation at the investors' office. Indeed, the militaries always provide an efficient service to the government. But there is no more time left, and the recording is being analyzed at the General Solicitor's office, where we could ear:

"According to the constitutional system of Canada, his document will take maybe one month before being accepted by Parliament. If it goes thru the system and becomes a White Book with the media and everything, in Britain for instance, we're done. And the President would be worst for us if he's aware of such a document. No more document, no more John Barlow, that's our goal!"

"Yeah. We better start taking care of John now or after the possible end of the war."

"There's no war. Let's act with our people and literally do something to have him down, necessarily, because if he's alive, we're still in trouble."

"I actually met that kid myself some years ago, and I know his tenacity.

Today, he's the wrong man in the wrong place. Too bad for him, if he had attended university, his document would have piled up like the others, and his life would have been safe. Yes, we'll get all our people and break that Parliament-Sussex Drive", 'this is certainly the voice of the US senator of the State of North Carolina.' After listening to the tape, the General Solicitor called the man who knows everything about Canada, the politicians and their families, the citizens, the army and anything else. This person, of course, a soldier, can tell you what your neighbor ate for supper last Friday. His name is CWO Marsh Glockhouse. There is categorically no secret for such a man. He's alone with the General Solicitor in the office, and their conversation is being recorded.

"What do you think about all this recording and its content?" the GS asked.

"The Prime Minister is in great danger, Sir. We have first-hand information about his problems with his political contacts", the Non-Commission Officer (NCO) is holding many sheets like they were notes.

"Tell me everything in detail...", the GS looked very interested.

"Since the assassination of his brother in law, Rev. Troy Wilson, we followed the PM until his rise to power. Apparently, the Reverend was killed because he wanted to push out the Prime Minister from the electoral race. Some people close to his family ordered the murder."

"What does this have to do with the recording in an office in New York?"

"The office in New York is controlled by a powerful American senator who is leading the group of the most important investors in the world. Now, for quite some time, the PM has been secretly working on a new revolutionary economic system base on Welfare Economics. The office in New York hacked his computer and copy the document. Mr. John Barlow proposed an operational plan to implement Welfare Economics in the systems of the world."

"The investors don't like the plan of the PM, I guess," the GS suggests.

"No, not at all Sir. In following him, we knew that because of his longtime business partner warned him about that. There are more important things than that... An important military task force was called to carry the PM's death..."

Glockhouse didn't finish what he was saying that many soldiers in full combat gear are knocking at the door's office. They're near the Parliament quarters - but they can't hear the gunshots. One of the soldiers hands a riffle to the veteran member of the army while saying: "the Parliament is being assaulted... helicopters, tanks..." They walked toward the exit door while the General Solicitor is on the phone with the army headquarters.

The streets are empty as if people did know everything about a killing squad coming in the Canadian capital. Several helicopters are part of the attack as a partial tactical mistake. One squadron is heading the area as many land units are rushed to provide a good defense. Now, colonel Thunders and his men are almost finished. Only rubbles can be seen in what used to be a national governmental headquarters. It's like the entire capital was burning instead of a one-kilometer radius area. Close to fifteen men are on the ground looking for John. Armed men from federal police corps, local regiments, and Parliament security forces are running everywhere trying to locate the PM. Since John's last conversation with the US senator, Pepper knew there was something suspicious. He called at Sussex Drive while John was at Parliament for the debate. The call was sent to Ann during her shopping at Ogilvie, in downtown Ottawa. Some seconds after that, Thunders' task force attacked. Ann is calling at Sussex Drive to warn about the immediate danger. She's leaving the store in panic as if she was hopeless. Two bodyguards are entering the car with her. She asks the driver to stop the vehicle her to go to the bathroom. The guards followed her as a security procedure. Passing the bathroom's door alone, Ann stayed inside just enough time to come out and escapes the bodyguards. She's taking the cab. Sitting in, she's telling the driver about her problems concerning the dramatic events that are presently happening at Sussex Drive and the Parliament. Ann is questioning him about his activities for the day. He's not doing anything.

"You're Mrs. Barlow, the Prime Minister's wife," the taxi driver said with surprise.

"Yes. They're shooting at Parliament! They're trying to kill my husband!"

"Who's trying to kill your husband?"

"Some killers!"

The driver accelerates the speed of the car. He's showing a lot of talent for stock car and Formula 1 racing. And probably a good member of the organization for the emergency drivers. Many lights and stops' signs are being crossed at one hundred miles. It's indeed a lucky day because the road security patrollers are absent. Although a great number of sirens of several emergency services could be heard from four to five miles away. Ann remains calm and worried at the same time. In her mind, she's thinking about a fifty percent chance of John's death. There is no difference between her and the probable widows of the 2nd World War. She would probably ask Mrs. Barbara Bush about the feeling of such terrible circumstances. The car is going faster. Some large weapons and explosive devices can readily be heard as the cab is approaching closer to Parliament Quarters.

Ann pulls her cell phone as she tells the driver to stop on the side of a street. She's calling John using a number that she's the only one on earth who knows. The parliamentary debate continues at the Canadian House of Parliament as the men of colonel Thunders are closing in to finish the job. A trained dog like Thunders will do precisely what he was asked. It looks like John's coffin is already closed and ready for the twenty-one gunshots for the death of a head of state. Indeed, somebody else than his former wife attempted to help JFK escaped his death by advising him as a premonition to avoid Dallas, Texas. This Canadian John sad story is already on another tone although the structure is the same. All kinds of ideas are in this particular John's wife's mind because she's intimately attached to him like a magnetized steel bar who joined in with a piece of metal. It's time now to answer the phone. He's addressing the parliamentarians on the war that just happened. And his deadly pursuers time already reached eleven minutes on fifteen. Thunders' helicopters are passing by the Supreme Court building. The longtime leading officer is about to punch some kind of a time card and retire peacefully from employment that is unequivocally not done for nobody. Every six to seven years old child wants to be a soldier. It's not always possible to discourage people from going to the army. Rommel told his son to never even think about following him. Bismarck exhorted his son to don't replace him at the service of the king. Apparently, John, Pepper, Thunders, the NC senator, the GS, CWO Glockhouse and William took the wrong job. These positions kill morality and the very crucial fiber of human spiritual life. John is answering his cell phone to enter a world where he has never been, and surely never imagined. His safety is threatened, but his plan was done some years ago when he bought his kingdom among mankind with his own money. Of course, history proves that Louis XVI, Napoleon, the Czar, and Marshal Petain had no HARD CASH. And especially today, most young women that worth something are not impressed at all by those salaried professionals. Also, in the governmental organisations, some individuals tend to mix their small resources with the organisation's big money by the cheating feeling of intimate attachment to a working place. All these people were fictitious dreamers without any practical means to contribute or to clear a good account. John is debating live on television. He's going somewhere at the back of the MP's seats and opens his cell phone.

"Ann darling, why are you calling me now? You know that…," John looked surprised.

"John, my dear, get out of the Hill now! Pepper called, and he said that some killers are after you. They're coming to Parliament and at the house to kill you."

The phone line suddenly breakdown as John is speaking with Ann. Several cars, Jeeps and trucks are part of the logistic of the large group of killers. All communications in the area close to the Parliament are strictly controlled as the waves are garbled. Cell phones are out of use. Colonel Thunders' men continue their action by firing shots from all kinds of weapons. The group is resuming their mission by killing policemen and guards repeatedly. Three special units of the Canadian Forces are entering the big gun battle. Some of the Thunders' men are already leaving while many others are on the ground searching for John Barlow. The Senator is calling John at his pretended unknown phone number.

"You still alive! It doesn't matter, you'll be dead later on anyway", the senator said as an attempt to break John's motivation.

"I can't believe this, you're part of all that craziness... Are you out of your mind?"

"You're out of your mind. It looks like you still ignore the financial consequences of your goddamn ideas! Think about it, you state in your document that the wage adjustments for the fifty million Americans that have an insufficient or inexistent salary would be two thousand five hundred billion dollars. The government doesn't have that kind of money. So, we would have to pay it with the investments' money. You got that!"

"Senator, I thought we had an agreement."

"You're dreaming kid! The stupid General Solicitor of yours will press charges against you... We had to let you down."

While John is speaking to the senator, Ann is calling him. He's taking the call.

"It's you darling?" John answered like he knew it was Ann.

"Where are you Johnny baby? They're shooting everywhere."

"I'm already out of the Hill. Can you see the blue car on the street, on your right? I'm in it."

"Yes! Hum..."

Every professional and experienced gunman always find a way to escape death. Knowing the army's method and members can make somebody thinks that it is possible to oppose one soldier against an entire nation. Colonel Thunders will be frustrated because he can't kill John Barlow. The phone line suddenly breakdown again. Now, Ann is running toward John. He's looking at the car's keys where it's written RCMP. Actually, the Crown Victoria is generally used by SWAT team members. Ann is embarking in the vehicle. John drives to an alley at the back of the stores. He's now opening the trunk looking for weapons. Again, just like the old days, John is happy because there areplenty of rifles and shotguns.

Several members from the killing group are running toward John as he's being identified. He's bringing two Heckler And Koch and a Styr Aug in front of the car with him. John stops in front of a fifteen floor building. Ann is entering the building as John is shooting the members of the killing group that is following him. He's taking the elevator with a bag packed with ammunition and the three rifles. There is a fierce and raging battle between the military units in charge of protecting the Parliament and the killing squad. For support and encouragement, Pepper is well informed of the situation, and he's running in, leading a group of policemen searching to protect John. Five to ten men from Thunders group is shooting on Pepper and the policemen. They're all dead. Ann is still in a panic. She's questioning John, and she's blaming him for everything.

"You're not going to tell me that you're as surprised as me to see all that is happening? I know for a fact that these people are not mysteriously trying to kill you. Sadder, they're butchering people only to get to you," Ann told John with remorse.

"I'll explain okay. Several years ago before our companies were well established, me and Pepper, we use to work for the underworld."

"Doing what? Killing people? Stealing?"

"Everything you can imagine. Let say that it's not the kind of job where you need to send in your resume... And now, one of our contacts, a wealthy US senator wants to kill me because of the document I wrote on the implementation of Welfare Economics in a liberal economy. You remember when I was printing the document..."

"He wants to kill you for that. The document is not even published or anything. I read it several times, and I think that it's convenient."

Although she didn't appreciate the quite big mess that he caused, she's lying with her head on his stomach. She probably feels that it's better to keep him strong instead of throwing negative ideas and words. As she rubs his shoulder, she approaches his face and kisses him. It's only a very short break because while they're hiding on the thirteenth floor, the killers are guessing by systematically searching the second.

Pepper and the policemen are outside in cover near some cars. The military police members are running toward the building. Many men from the death squad are already inside. Now, a high-rank military of the Canadian Forces recognizes Colonel Thunders when they had to destroy Pepper's fortress in the Laurentians.

"Colonel Thunders, you're not supposed to be against us! Who issued you the order to come here?" the officer said like a peace agreement.

"Who cares? I'm here to burn your damn ass!"

The colonel is telling his sniper to shoot the high-rank officer. A huge caliber bullet passed thru his bare head as he falls dead instantly. Pepper runs toward the officer like he was going to help him. He approaches the dead man as a sergeant is mumbling:

"He did too many delicate missions. Yeah! Men like that always die ugly."

"Have you been on these missions with him?" Pepper asked.

"Of course, most of them! We weren't soldiers anymore, we were a killing squad just like the criminals."

"Did you ever had to kill criminals? I mean the drug busts or kind of things like that."

"Yeah! Sure. Everything. We actually destroy a quite big fortress here with the man that you just saw, Colonel "Hyena" Thunder."

"Oh yeah! Hum... Wow. It's sad to assist the death of a warrior who is your friend."

Pepper looks like he's trying to keep his emotions. He's running with the other policemen in the direction of Colonel Thunders and his killers. There is a big fire-fight. Most of the killers are dead. Colonel Thunders is entering the building like he knew that John is hiding there. Pepper gets inside by the front. The noises of the bullets are very high. Since he didn't succeed yet in killing John Barlow, he didn't leave although his time has passed. Some of the men of the group did go. Colonel Thunders stayed to become the death of John became a personal business. He's now alone against all the law and order forces. The hunter is presently a prey.

John is hiding in an office on the thirteenth floor. The colonel stops by the fifth floor as two of his men are agonizing. Colonel Thunders is talking to the men's. One of them mumbles: "the bastard PM is on the thirteenth floor." Thunders is heading up with his weapon ready to shoot. As he passes by the office where John and Ann are hiding, John seems to know that somebody is on the floor. John opens the door and finds himself on the corner of another alley facing the back of the colonel.

"Hold it! Don't move! Drop your weapon!" The colonel let his FAMAS the submachine gun falls on the floor and lifts both hands up.

The elevator stops and the doors open. Pepper is looking carefully while pointing his pistol and rifle at every direction. He feels relieved when he turns the corner of the alley and sees John aiming firmly at the colonel with a loaded Styr Aug riffle. They tie up the colonel as some other policemen come on the floor searching everywhere for possible members of the group. The policemen confirmed that the building is clear - so safe regarding security. John opens the door of the office and takes Ann in his arms. Then both three friends-family hold on together as tears come out of their eyes.

"We're lucky to be alive. Again, we're the winners," John said happily to Pepper.

"Yes, we won!"

"Just like in the old tale, Candid, from the French writer, Voltaire: 'everything is for the better in the best of the worlds.'"

John looks at Ann and takes his right arm around her hips as she leans her head on his chest. They get in the elevator with some other people that work in the building along with some policemen. When coming out of the building, several journalists already gather into a big pile. Some family members, Mary, Jessica, Alex, and Jesse, are there. It's a big reunion.

In the first weeks following the violent incidents at Parliament, the General Solicitor of Canada tried to issue a subpoena against PM John Barlow. The Chief Judge of the Canadian Supreme Court never signed such a document for insufficient physical evidence. Even the

North Carolina senator couldn't be charged in the US, nor in Canada. This Canadian-US secret service-military imbroglio left some hard stains on one man only, Colonel Remy "Hyena" Thunders, who was released after his extradition to the United States because he "acted under military orders." After the significant grief suffered by Canada with the destruction of its governmental headquarter and the death of so many citizens, the two North-American governments reached an accord of some three billion dollars and some public excuses at the International Court of Lahaie on October the 23rd 1997.

After a short period, in a very crowded hall of the United Nations building in New York, PM John Barlow presented his implementation plan for Welfare Economics in the economies of the world. All the countries of the four continents agreed to the ideas of John. The only obstacle, a quite small one, is that human labour force needs to be taken entirely out from the production of goods and services. The committees of the UN felt that it is challenging to balance a group that is working from another who doesn't have to provide anything. Again, it was because of the misunderstanding of a part in John's document where it is specified that the more technology we will have, the better it will be for a world base on Welfare Economics. The UN accepted John's document and they created a world super-government of twenty-five hundred members that will coordinate the construction of facilities, autoroutes, and all kinds of things that materialistically would satisfy everybody. It's been estimated that after a maximum time of a decade, each and every person on the planet will have the living standard of a millionaire.

John is sitting at his personal house's office, and he thinks that it never came in his mind that he would be a scientist. He feels comfortable to be an ordinary citizen. Bill Barlow, his father, never did communicate that social standing of a professional to him. How could it be so? People are fooling their surrounding with an image. In John's mind, his father and some other members of his family knew all the details about his future. In some ways, they didn't want him to be a progressive or left wing person because they're diabolic and illogical. But it's still the mysteries of life to don't know exactly how many things that people are hiding from him - and why. He knows for a fact that people see things and have knowledge that is not written in the significant number of books that he read. In fact, he can't counter a stupid circus that is driven by some rules which are not noted nowhere accessible to him.

His accomplishment of implementation of Welfare Economics in the world for every human being is unreal and have no effect on the deep mysteries of life. The reason is that people are trying to make him think that they're acting blindly. When in fact, they, his father, uncle, cousins, mother, William, Pepper and all kinds of other people, see from a place that is utterly close to John Barlow's eyes.

CHAPTER 10

John is thinking about leaving the political scene forever. He will indeed never forgot all that apprenticeship as a Prime Minister. Nothing is complicated in life. He knows that he just have to take what he wants. People oppose themselves to the ones that wish so. All opponents agree to be in such a position. In other words, there is no such thing as hazardous events. A person always conforms to what happened in his everyday life. Of course, if you don't think about controlling your life, you'll have the impression that you don't have any power on the events that are happening to you. John is happier than before he was Prime Minister. Everything looks so simple for him now. The probably hidden secrets of life are being revealed to him in a way that any scholar would have ignored.

Ann and probably all the people surrounding John Barlow are comforted about the fact that he doesn't fit in any of the regular clichés that usually is associated with a prominent politician. His dark past of bank-robber and gang member didn't follow him. John knows very well why he's continuously evolving. The reason is that he never does anything without a specific purpose. Phrasing the profound truth about life can be different from one individual to another one. John always says and think this way: "there is nothing more sacred than the will of an individual. The will of a person stops him from agreeing to other ideas, no matter how true they are. The truth is that there is no truth – apart from all what you made up in your thoughts which is the real thing."

Without being a scientist, John said once that "there are no uncontested scientific facts; everything is subject to change depending on the will." Of course, John is like one of these ordinary citizens who knows plenty of things on their own that are probably written in some books. Since he reads a lot, he surely learned it in some books.

Like in his economic program, John Barlow started to attract the attention of some people. With the exception that this time, he's more dedicated. About half of the population of the world has been waiting for Jesus-Christ for quite sometimes as it was biblically announced. And we also have individuals who have only questions: what will happen in the next years or so on this earth; what is the real fundamental nature of human beings; and some other mysteries.

The idea of John about the sacredness and the power of an individual's will is quite essential for the comprehension of human life mysteries. In the application of John's thoughts, our afterlife is what we want it to be if we decide to die. There are no "uncontested scientific facts" would mean that somebody doesn't necessarily die at a certain age or at a certain point of time. Even if it does happen that people pass away when they get ancient, there is a strong possibility of a change. Will these changes occurred overnight or after a long period? Unless his statement or assumption is completely false with no practical effect. Several personalities came to visit John in Ottawa discussing with him on all kind of subjects. The latest two persons who came to see John was a writer from Africa. A quite strange individual who reveals him a lot of things that he didn't know. Although the author confirms the idea of John that "the truth is that there is no truth," he opposed himself about the existence of "uncontested scientific facts."

"John, the world has this fundamental aspect that it can be formed the way we want it to be. It is not yet a question that everything has a fixed nature. Even though it's been proven that the general will can't be applied to the ones who refuse it. In other words, the world is not a group - the world doesn't exist. There are numerous little worlds as the same number of human beings," the writer told John like some kind of a great philosopher.

"So our power as a leader is not real. Since several individuals voted against their will," John replied with a lack of understanding of the writer's statement.

"Actually, people are never aware of their high capacity. They don't need any leader. We often tend to think that they need each other. They are with who they want to be without any obligation or needs," the writer felt an urgency to bring more ideas.

"To be honest with you, I think I feel some guilt in my position. I mean, am I retaining people against their will...?"

"No, you're doing what you have to do and what you want to do. If people don't want to support you in your task, it's merely their own decision. You don't have, or you can't do nothing about it. Instead of losing your time, you got better things to do for yourself."

The writer was some kind of an encouragement advisor for John Barlow. There was something bizarre though, he never read the books of this author. So Mr. Ayofan Batianbe gave him a copy of an essay, Seeing the Invisible, and a novel, The Eternal Joy. Both of the books are best-sellers. Then John said to Mr. Batiambe: "we can read a million books without reading all that is being written." Mr. Batiambe said that "we can know all the disciplines, but we can't practice them all."

Everything starts to look like, at the end of a political mandate, a man becomes wiser as to if he was at the end of his life. The dinners, the friendly get-togethers, and other reunions always bring the same people: John's family, Wesley's, Lexington's, William's and all the advisors and else. The other important fact is that none of the people surrounding John have less than $100 million. In the case of the African author, his father left something like $800 million for him, his two sisters and their little brother. Most of the simple millionaire that John knew at the beginning of his career keep very far from him. If some situations link some people together, money just separates them. Is it the style of life? Not at all. A $100 million individual can have the same hobby as a $5 million, with the difference that they don't mix well because their fortune will never be the same.

John's business partners and advisors are already preparing his future after he leaves office. An investment strategy company in Ottawa is already talking of some $20 billion for John in the third year after he leaves his position. As a strange and fortunate event, more people with more money is gathering around him like bees and honey. More happiness also because Ann has never loved him more than at the present peak of power and monetary wealth.

They gathered at the country house in the Great Lakes region. John, Westley and some high profile people from the Western governments met to discuss some financial issue in the US. In the evening, Pepper sat down with John, and the question was about what his father left for him. Actually, Westley wanted to tell John about all what he picked up in Houston, the things his father left him.

"Yeah, there were two letters where my dad stated that I must contact several individuals who are able to bring some ninety tons of platinum from outer space and forty tons of gold he found in Yugoslavia."

"And, did it work. You contacted these people to get the treasures."

"Indeed, I called them as my father told me in the letters."

"You mean, you took possession of all that money."

"Of course, the total amount I got from the exchange of all that stockpile of gold and platinum was 7.4 trillion dollars. I gotta tell you that I already started the costly process of taking care of my public image."

"You're already the greatest businessman in North-America. What do you want more?"

"Maybe you're right, John. I feel there's always something more we're looking forward to owning."

John feels that people often talk against the cash but on the other hand, none of them will give you at least $10 thousand when they have $100 million. He started to think that money is the essence of life on earth if you don't have enough or not at all, you'll die. About a month before John called some new elections, his company made a considerable investment, $3 billion in four new stocks that are apparently good for the next year or so. The people in charge of the company have decided that even if the stocks keep on rising, at ten dollars, they will sell. A reasonable investor needs to be where the action is at the right moment. By putting their hands on these stocks, the positive results are almost automatic. Although it looks like anybody can come out of nowhere to buy a stock and become very rich, this is entirely false in real life. You need to know and to control all the people that are involved in the markets and all the financial activities on the planet if not in Canada and the U.S.A. only. There is no justice in all that economics imbroglio. John makes a lot of money because he controls and pays everybody: his stocks are not rising by chance. The process by which some vast fortunes are made is full of guilty people. John makes all kind of phone calls to some essential individuals or organizations, and they've been cultivating a long-term friendship. Failing in such a situation is impossible. In other words, to make a bad investment.

Also, money is a sign of intelligence: a person is smart when he sees the importance of the cash. Especially in our quite technologically advanced world, there is nothing more powerful and easy to carry than money. A person can't bring some very high quantity of goods and services, but he can bring billions with him anywhere. Some poor people are dishonest or too stupid to see and recognize a fact. For example, Ann is not a materialistic person, but she did appreciate a lot the million dollar diamond necklace John bought for her.

"Oh my God, this is wonderful! John, Honey! Where did you get that."

"I bought it in a big jewelry store. My eyes got so huge when I saw it, and I suddenly thought about you. Since it's not a question of money, I took it for you," John said with a seductive tone in his voice.

Jewelry and lovely expensive gifts have a powerful effect on a couple. Indeed, it helps keep the couple together. There is no such thing like a husband that doesn't cherish his wife with flower and gifts. And most couples are successful because of the significant revenues that come into the household. In the relationship between Ann and John, we can really see the power of cash to bring marital bliss. He was already a millionaire when she married him. The most interesting is that his money was hidden. And, it is evident that this money provided confidence in his attitude. If we look at all the people that are close to John, we see only money. Even the American colonel Lane Perry that Lexington invited for dinner at his house in suburban Ottawa is not poor at all. His family is one of the most prosperous African-American family. Perry has close or more than $80 million. in his bank accounts. Together, these people can buy one if not two continents.

CHAPTER 11

National leaders meet so many different people that they become very experienced and intelligent. In this regard, John met several Third-world country leaders. It is sad to see the horrors that a simple lack of cash can cause to reasonable human beings. The miseries of these people are quite astounding. Also, their leaders seem to live in an imaginary world where they lose control with reality.

The head of State of some Caribbean countries met with John in Ottawa to discuss financial assistance. The Parliament has agreed to distribute some $7 HUNDRED BILLION to six countries: Jamaica, Trinidad & Tobago, Haiti, St-Maarten, St-Lucia, and the Dominican Republic. John took the time to talk extensively with some of the leaders. The President of Jamaica told John that he appreciates the economic help a lot along with all the citizens of his country. John didn't know that the Jamaican President is a millionaire himself at birth. Mr. Antony Johnson lived in New York for ten years before he got back to Jamaica. Now, President Johnson and his family worth $2 BILLION. He's frank with his citizens, in the sense that he always gives a clear account of his government's activities.

On the other hand, the President of Haiti, Mr. Monberlin Celeste, is an ex-high apparatchik of the World Bank who was never satisfied with his salary. He grew up without his father in an impoverished family. The fact that the President of Haiti wasn't his personal wish but only a yes word to some friends that asked him. So the day he received the $950 millions from Ottawa, he made a deposit in his own bank account to become a billionaire. He hid everything by making some loans and launching false works to rebuild the country to keep everything going for the next two years before he leaves office with his money. John talked to him before he left Ottawa:

"I went to George Washington University and then to Cambridge where I did my D. Sc. People like me because of my ideas in economics. In fact, I'm a simple man who doesn't give a damn about anything. I like to have my cash to live a good life by buying all the expensive and glamorous things that I need to fill my life with happiness and glory," Mr. Celeste told John.

"Why is it that you don't care about nobody? I mean people are not that bad."

"Why should I worry about people? However, if they do care for me, they're losing their time. I don't see why I should care about anybody except myself," Mr. Celeste said to John like he had never been in power in any country. The personal point of view of such a man shows the illusion of political responsibility. John feels like Canada should have never given money to a state with such a President. Even if he doesn't have any proof of wrongdoing with government's funds, he just doesn't trust Mr. Celeste. Since it's a private conversation, John will not reveal anything to the press. After all, Mr. Celeste is not that different from the normal process by which dishonest people get to power.

John knows very well that Canada is not different from any other third-world country with social injustice. Regarding proportion, Canada has more millionaire than the U.S.A. The wealthy Canadian families that John and Westley met to give more strength to their financial empires control more than a third of the country's wealth. Although the history of the Canadian dynasties is inspiring for people that wish to become rich one day, under the surface, there are some very troubling facts for the country's democratic reputation. Actually,

John and Westley are part of those worrisome facts. For somebody that knows the political history of Canada very well, John and Wesley did copy on the practices of many Canadian dynasties. He's trying to remember the rest of his conversation with the African author, who quotes Nietzsche in a very imaginative way, by stating that there is evidence that each and every person in an entire nation can become a billionaire." Friedrich Nietzsche said that "the person that climbs the highest mountains mocked himself of allreal or simulated tragedies." It is clear that even though Nietzsche said a logical phrase, he didn't have enough scientific insight to see the practical means of it. " In my opinion, Nietzsche blindly indicated that there is an invisible system that transfers all messages. For example, a person that is climbing Everest is smart enough to send the message that he's capable of doing it by never worry or do anything that makes understand that he can't get to the top. In Nietzsche's personal life, we can see the anxiety and some other problems that surprise us from a man who wrote all the solutions with the exception that he didn't understand them," Mr. Batiambe told John.

John is thinking that maybe we can start sending messages about all the things that we want, like a cure for cancer, new technologies to go on the other planets and more. But he's asking himself if he ever did send a message himself to become a multibillionaire Prime Minister - Unconsciously, of course. In fact, we know all the effort he applies to rob banks at gunpoint, which was a clear indication of his burning desire to be very rich someday. Actually, he never stops any activity that would bring him a lot of money. After the criminal activities, he legalizes his cash and invests it riskily without any fear. There is also the personal idea of John that money is the key to every door. For John, this is the truth. Although a lot of people don't share such an opinion.

He went to his room and took a sheet of paper where he wrote:

"People are often scared to choose what they want. They feel like driving an expensive car or live some kind of a glamorous life in a castle, but they're there, hesitating. Why? They still won't admit the supremacy of money. And the worse is that they want to travel to some far away country, they never did because they don't have the cash. There is also a terrible news for them: they can make all the efforts in the world, if they can't pay in hard cash, they won't get nothing."

John is all dressed up. It is time to go, Ann is ready. They are invited to a party with some of the wealthiest in the world. He has the strange feeling to drive the car, but Ann doesn't want him to take the steering. "Why you want to drive, darling? May I ask you to don't do such a thing," Ann doesn't want him to worry about anything like a driver does.

"Come on, I want to drive our beamer!"

"John, my dear, you've passed that stage of things... like touching steering. If you want to know, my most-precious-one, I'm totally opposed to that."

"Ah... Ah... Ah! You find that driving is something...! You must be joking."

"I'm very serious! Jessica! Call Bron and tell him I want him to drive us."

"Mummy! Dad already told him he doesn't..."

Sometimes people tend to lose memory or their sense to keep being what they are. An essential man like John who can buy half of the world wants to drive his automobile. It is time for a woman with a mental sharpness to tell him to never even think of doing such a thing, which is entirely improper to a powerful multibillionaire.

John is still thinking about that rapper he saw in New York who was saying:

"When somebody makes me a promess, I blast!
When somebody tells a story, I shoot live!
When somebody give me a check, I smash!
If you pay me in hard cash, you'll live forever!

Every time I blast, it was the same thing!
Money, money, pay me or die!
Some friends passed away for the debts.
If you owe me, I will erase you forever!

Last time I pulled out, both falls without recovery,
And I'm still close to cause some burial services.
It's still quite sad that people can't pay,
While at the same time, there is no coffin.
If you bring my hard cash, I'll hand you tricks.

People won't pay their debts until death.
Another reason for all stories to be misfortunate.
Hey man! I wanted everything to be good.
If they were alright, my bell wouldn't be on the face.

He was thinking that sadness is all around searching for another victim to make the headlines. Everything seems to be gloomy for the ones who owe money. Maybe this artist doesn't have anything to do with his piece of poetry. He was probably just translating the message of nature. It's certainly not the kind of things that he needs right now. Life has stopped for John Barlow even if he's alive with his wife and the big fortune. He's so attached to ordinary things like driving his automobile and walking on the street like an unknown person. John is unquestionably now a man who can't carry himself properly. All that he represents is too heavy. The man is so blind about his size that he thinks that anybody can be like or is the same as him. It's completely false. Some two to three billions of spectators around the world watched him for the speech at the UN. Why he between the six billion humans on the planet had to be viewed with so much admiration. He can't and will never understand the fact that he's a great man. The concept of greatness never entered his mind the right way. It's like the Dean of the university who presented Dr. Frederick Banting in a way that the inventor of diabetic medication, never catch. The applause and the fascination of the public completely froze the Canadian scientist with extreme shyness. The lesson is hard to learn for personalities to know that they're different from the crowd.

CHAPTER 12

Several weeks have passed, and John is going to New York with Pepper, William and the retired general Lexington for the appointment of Colonel Lane Perry as general and commander of the US Joint Chief of Staff. Perry's name is also there at the race for the Senate in California. John and probably many well-known figures of the world political intelligentsia know perfectly the danger represented by Perry at any high-level position in the US government. In the US, nobody has ever taken seriously the power of leaders to be the object of too much fascination. Perry is a proud imperialist who comes from a family with several army members who were highly decorated, and he intends to keep the tradition alive by enforcing a robust military agenda in the country. The Marines commander is also a great admirer of the World War II winner, General George Smith Patton. What Perry likes most is the idea of Patton, after the German's defeat, to continue the US military advance deep into Russian territory. This wasn't possible because the general in chief, Eisenhower, refused. It is his goal and dream to do what his ancestor and model, general Patton had in mind his effort to drill an entire nation behind his idea to conquer the world, he's making speeches almost everywhere like an electoral leader. As a strange coincidence, people started to like him since his little defeat against the Russian commando in Alaska. His commanders thought of risking him because he was already a colonel at a young age. No danger for him to don't become a general some day. Now, in every part of the U.S.A., Perry is known and respected for his moral and his dedication to lead the country firmly. But, even in the US constitution, there are articles to protect the nation from the dangerous all-powerful leaders. Everything indicates that it's too late at this moment to stop Perry. The military leader intends to resign his top position at the Joint Chief of Staff to be able to run for the Senate where he will surely win. Technically, he can't be out of the army. He merely needs to do something that will free and enable him to go in the Senate election race.

On his part, John Barlow went to Perry's appointment because of his friends, Pepper and Lexington. It's mysterious, but he knows all about Perry's political agenda. And, he doesn't agree to most of the contents. John and many other experienced politicians are sure that the U.S.A. is on their way to a devastating dictatorship under Perry's command as President. Suddenly, the world and its events are moving at a fast pace. Many countries, Japan, Germany, France, Turkey, are already mumbling about pulling out their consent from NATO. At the same time, they are well aware of the danger of not following the Americans. Strategically, none of the European countries can afford the price of a destabilized continent like theirs. In all cases, Perry can pursue his imperialistic goals safely because, at the first objection, he knows what to do to keep everybody calm. The new general is not a man who likes group, apart from the army. He wants to have "Pepper" as a military leader and William as his first political and governmental advisor. He thinks that as soon as he accomplishes such a mix, the rest of the world, according to him, belongs to America. Another reasonable assumption is that Perry's opposition with John can be fatal for his presidency. He's not able to make the distinction between leading and conquering the world. For John, it's one more great battle. Perry thinks he can have the upper hand on John because of all the delicate pieces of information that American secret services have on the Canadian PM.

On the other hand, "Pepper" will have to choose between obeying to his commander and keep his friendship with John. Although Perry has less international contacts than John, the political fight is still tight, and there is no definite winner. John is smart enough to stop any escalation by inviting his opponent to a world electoral race. Most importantly, he must avoid a regional conflict Canada-U.S.A. Now, he needs to use his American political contacts to put himself on the podium and open up that fist fight against Perry.

When he went to the party with Ann, several key figures of the world international high finance told him to watch his step. It's not that they're not ready to support him. They want to be free to choose the most profitable world leader. Should it be Perry or John? Nobody cares. Two days after that party, John put two of the most prominent offices in public and political matters under contract to study the problem and send the results to him. On the other side, Perry kept pressuring on NATO and the WARSAW PACT members to be obedient to him if they don't want to suffer. The Marines commander have the intention to use the same tactic with John.

Fundamentally, Perry didn't do anything else than destabilizing the world affairs politically. NATO itself has been under question because of the British thought that Turkey would be of a greater defense use than France to stop enemy troops from the east side. Now, everything becomes worst with Perry trying to take these countries' independence. He wants to have the upper hand on all matters in every part of the world by centralizing more the entire planet on America. In such a condition, there will be a better ground for capitalism to flourish than it has never been in the history of mankind. So, now there is Perry the capitalist and John, the Welfare Economics enforcer. Who will win this time?

Perry doesn't know anything about the kind of political system that he's encouraging. He's just a sick-minded military who he's at the peak of his discipline, which brought him to become a serious and the most dangerous power tripper known to man. It was like when Rome was at the head of the world, its dictators were savagely conquering and concentrating the resources to cause the suffering of many humans. Today, even in a functional democracy, the attention is focused on Perry. Whatever he said is considered as the truth. An entire nation and some other key groups in the world are mesmerized by him. Will people wake up and see the troubling beast inside such a man?

Nothing looks good because in Russia, several months before Perry became general, Vladimirovich Igor Vatievski was named to lead the Third Army Corps, a significant component of their Armed Forces. The ex colonel from the missing invasion In Alaska is well informed about Perry, and he doesn't like him at all. As the Russians are preparing themselves for war along with the Americans who are ready, the other NATO and WARSAW PACT countries don't want to participate in any conflict. Nobody didn't say anything yet, but there is a strong feeling that most of these countries will withdraw their consent from their respective group defense organization.

Even Canada, under the command of John, will not surely agree to Perry's demand like some States in the U.S.A. The difference is that it wouldn't be surprising if Canada goes with Russia, which would be a great strategy to stop Perry. But what about Perry's good financial backup? With all these people who are ready to be with him because he's promoting a system that offers all-powerful protection for their fortune.

The situation of the world looks so critical for the near future that many influential people are worried as they're questioning themselves about the terror days predicted in the Bible. Has the world just arrived at the messianic times? The humans are backing up to the period of the vassals where wars were killing the poor as most of the other peoples would live in a constant agonization. Since John is still alive, intelligence and science will prevail. Nobody has to follow any prophecy because Perry is merely insane and unscientific. The future President doesn't have any point at all.

Some four days before the election date for the Senate in California,

John pays a visit to the next President. Perry is very careful with John as with all the personalities that encountered him before. The superior military officer knows well enough that John wants to make sure he's someone trustful. For now, Perry is treating John the best way possible until he gets to the presidency.

"I guess you about to become the next President of the U.S.A.," John said as he smiled.

"Probably, but for now we'll take it one at a time and slowly. The Senate in California and then we'll see." Perry is in the Marines parade dress, white and blue. And he looks very calm and focused. He wouldn't be a psychopath because he's using a lot of intelligence to make sure that anything that is not American remains crushed under his foot.

"I mean there is nothing to hide. You'll be the next President very soon, after the current mandate."

Perry is by the window of his office and looking outside with his hand rubbing his jaw. And then, he violently states to John:

"Not so fast John! This is not like one of your Canadian elections. Apart from that, I'm stunned that you're still talking like before the attack on your Parliament. Look, John, I may be a moral man, but nothing has changed. I can be appointed to any other thing outside of any control and will."

"So the next presidency is yours as I understand."

"You didn't get it. All that is a mask for some other things."

"What are these other things? Tell me, I want to know."

"In about a month, our troops will be in Russia. Now you can either walk with us or lose. I strongly recommend you to be with us. If not, Canada will be considered as an enemy."

"What else should the US want? Russia has a liberal economy."

"I guessed that some people who are leading... have decided that it wasn't enough." "Sorry, but I have to tell you no from the part of Canada and myself. We don't agree to be part of that."

"Pepper is part of it! You won't follow your longtime business partner? And, not only that, you're a criminal... Your goddamn country made you a criminal! The PM that you think you are is only an image. I guess that if you didn't shoot anybody, you would be nothing."

"Let suppose I accept... our nuclear weapons on both side will erase us all."

"I think I know... this idea of total destruction comes from Dr. Robertson. Don't even talk about this idiot, he's dead and buried."

John is mistakenly feeling that Perry is trying to pressure him. In fact, he never did look forward to having John unwillingly on his side. He has too much respect for the Canadian PM. Actually, Perry knows "Pepper." better and because of that, he tried to be as friendly as possible with John. The truth of what Perry said made him feel a little bit uncomfortable. As a smart man, he accepted it and thought that his country cheated on him. Indeed, John knows that nothing will ever be the same in Canada and probably in the entire world.

The meeting is about to finish. Then Perry pulls out a file from the big stack of paper on his office. He's looking at it as John stares him reading the data. With ahigh pitch voice, Perry says:

"To tell you the truth, this is the man we're looking for. Vladimirovich Igor Vatievski, born in Siberia, finishes second at the Military

Academy, under the command of Captain Loubov. You have to understand that they were thirty-five officers in the class, and they're all with him in the plan to nationalize everything in Russia."

"Why? He's the commander in Alaska that didn't want to play the game."

"You're right. Some people can be severe for nothing."

"Now, they don't like him just as my Welfare Economics plan. Surely, Vatievski is about to jeopardize the quite big Russian market."

"Goddamn it, you're fast. You just got all that so fast. The danger is that hundreds of thousands of troops are under his command and his many support in the army."

"And the D-day is in a month. What about if this Vatievski or anybody else decides to play around with the mass destruction weapons?"

"The fight is entirely conventional. Some countries of NATO and the Warsaw Pact already made the diplomatic arrangements to take control of their arsenal and ours."

In his head, Perry is confident that John still ignores many tricky things. For instance, any treaty or diplomatic agreement is complete nonsense. The goal is to win by all means possible. Now, Perry thinks that there is always an idealist to come shake the peace of mind of the world, most of all, his own ease and comfort. He feels being dragged into a war that could have been avoided if most people were worried about their personal situation instead of the group. Everybody can take care of themselves. The violent revolutions caused by these generous dreamers didn't bring nothing constructive at all. And, in a month, he should win easily to bring the world back to its regular pace.

John knows that even if Perry didn't say it, he remains the champion who never lost. Pepper is excellent with some small defeats. They're both convinced that John can be on the battlefield as a high-rank officer just like them. Psychologically, John already abandoned his country for the fact that he feels betrayed by his family, father, mother, wife, except for the kids. It's too much for a man who's been living on this side of the world so many years.

In fact, Pepper himself knows since quite a long time that there is something strange with John. He talked to Perry about it once. Then they both came to the conclusion that they must not jump on false assumptions about John. If there is something significant, it will disentangle by itself. The primary hypothesis was his beautiful family surrounding. Why would a boy leave an excellent learning atmosphere in a remote Province to come doing crime in a big corrupted city? So his parents didn't know what was good for him. Richard Nixon was a good country student in Woodier, California. The same thing could have happened to John. He demonstrated many times his high cognitive skills. John is not a sinful man at all because he did everything they correctly showed him and he succeeded every time. Another excellent thing from John is that he's continuously searching for a moral which doesn't exist - in his mind maybe. He's even terribly lost sometimes because there are so many people who are doing the opposite of what has been prescribed. The fact is that John has to be the great leader who should set the rules - probably.

With the Governor, John had to deal or face some hard facts. Bill and Margaret's turn is coming slowly but surely. What did they hide from their son? Nobody would want to know. Some people have things concerning them that should remain secret. But greatness is about finding an impossible solution to a mystery. Indeed, many spent their lives without knowing who they were. It's not even a question of winning an election this time, but a real war. John is living in the body and mind of Perry, and he feels everything about the vast military challenge which is about to take place.

Perry thinks that if the Russians are encouraged to confront the US, there would be something to fear. If it's only Vatievski, he doesn't have nothing to worry about. The strategy of the new general is based on two principles: all the Russian army won't follow Vatievski because he's not paying and the population has no importance. Russian forces headquarters will conclude that there is no winning advantage for them. Vatievski's goal to stay as an honorable soldier in the line of a duty that his superiors already lied about is definitely futile. Again, America appeared, as mysterious as it would look, like being the ideal. In his head, he knows what his country is all about. And, it's undoubtedly not nationalism. It's a land to prosper where ever you may come from. And, there is a significant theological truth that comes with it.

The day after John talked to Perry. He's with Reverend Elijah Thompson who was forced to resign from his congregation because of corruption. John is surprised that Thompson didn't give him a call to see what can be done to arrange the problem. He knows that the Reverend probably felt more uncomfortable than before about the faith in the Gospel. But when finding himself face to face with John, the situation changes completely. Now, he thinks that Jesus is coming back. And Thompson's conviction is a little bit like a drug addict who needs a boost sometimes to keep being alive. Although the coming war against Russia is on every lip, he barely read about it.

"You resign from the Office. What are you going to do now?"

"I guess, I'll retire."

"What about a position in the government?"

"Maybe."

"You know what? I'm thinking about a meeting with the Russians to stop all this war threat between our two countries."

"I can be there with you."

"Okay, I'm calling Perry."

John is not sure if Perry wants such a meeting. The President might agree - in which case, Perry would reconsider his position toward the Russians. But for now, the war is the most likely thing. The basis for any conflict in the world is to try to be fair. A permanent rich person knows that he needs to always take his millions and never worry about anything. There is a good reason for that: everybody is being paid, and the name of the game is to have more money than the neighbor. No matter how low it is, there is a paycheck for each and every person. Perry is sure that Vatievski doesn't understand the situation the way he and John see it. In all cases, if Perry doesn't succeed in showing his tremendous strength to his opponent, his career and everything else are over. So, if John wants to discuss with Vatievski to cut a deal, it's his initiative. Perry doesn't want to be part of that. Last orders from the Pentagon to the US advance party of more than a hundred thousand men based in Europe indicate that the soldiers must carry their weapons, along with the live training exercises. The only thing that John can expect from Perry is to order Vatievski to resign and stop his plan for nationalism.

When putting everything in the right place or in the proper context, the side at fault should be shown. Perry, not the actual President is representing the US, gives an image of somebody who's defending something personal that will influence many people's lives. On the other side, Vatievski made a technical coup against the Russian government with his tremendous leadership on the army. He's mostly a well-armed idealist. For Perry, there is nothing to expect from the opponent. The troops will be in Russia, and they will win. After Perry's necessary appointments, there was much surprising news. For instance, some four weeks before, Chief Justice Douglas Matsber showed a very significative modification in the US constitution when declaring that legally the President is not just the supreme commander of the armed forces but the leader who has the power on all decisions. Technically, the judiciary head means that the legislative and all the order components surrounding the US government are only suggestive institutions: they study, they write, and they propose. The president will just decide of all applicability. The usual and old habit of Congress to vote became now some kind of professional advice where everybody raises their hands to help find the best logic. Obviously, for the first time in history, the US is clearly a dictatorial system or a loaded rifle in the only hands of a status quo.

The Third Army Corps that Vatievski is leading regroup everything that worth something in Russia. Most of the distinguished members of government come from this particular part of the army. For quite sometimes, things became worst for the reason that the person who leads the Third Army Corps is considered as the next or the actual president of Russia.

John never thought that the meeting with General Vatievski would come so fast. The Office of International affairs contacted the UN in New York to present a plan to the Russian government who is already broken apart. Most of the militaries who were there when the order was to invade the two North-American countries by Alaska had prepared everything to bring Vatievski to power. It happened to like The night of long knives of the Nazi government - with the exception that the Russian civilian leaders resigned and abandoned their governmental positions to free the way for the Great Officer. They informed John that they're ready to meet him or precisely Vatievski accepts to talk about the way he sees the world.

Perry declined to go with John. Not because the place is in Russian territory, the controversial city of Kiev. John didn't propose such a situation. The main reason why the Marines commander felt comfortable about his purposely absence from the 'negotiations' is that an extremely secret meeting took place between Vatievski and the ex-General who was in charge of the invasion by Alaska. The veteran officer of the red army warned the future President of Russia that being at the top leading position in the country is not a guaranty that they will win a war against the west. It was said that the US would be cautious in front of an imminent Russian attack because of the strategical consideration that the red army never bluff. But on the opposite, if they're not sure about a victory, they better ignore any belligerent idea against America. John doesn't know about all that, but he thinks of asking Vatievski to take some cash like many if not all the leaders who were considered as a menace to the world's financial and business stabilization. The amount of money was set as one and a half billion dollars for him only. While all the arrangements effort is going on to bring the world to peace, Perry is seriously preparing himself for war.

He met with all the US high-rank officers to show the way he wants to conduct the possible or maybe coming conflict. It's not that the officers do not agree to fight or totally opposed themselves to the war. They merely look at it as a patriotic and reasonably paid job. Perry starts by stating loudly:

"We don't want you, commanders, to take decisions on the battlefield. We want you to do what you were told by carrying the drills, all the drills and nothing else."

"That's what we always do...," one of the commanders answered.

"I'm not too sure about it... Look! Some fifty-three well trained special NATO soldiers died in Alaska and a great number of equipment like planes, helicopters, tanks... I personally called HQ to request some Marines units because I know what difference it would make. To tell you the truth, if it were Marines only, we would have precisely assessed the situation and recognized a great deal of difficulty to remove five hundred special Russian troops from their positions. My superiors would have accepted to wait before charging. I don't know who lost some of our wars... It's certainly not us. Listen, some years ago when we left Lebanon because the government couldn't clarify its policy..."

"What difference does it make? Now we can charge because of our advantage regarding equipment and better training!"

"You're goddamn right! From Russia, we'll open the way thru all the Warsaw Pact countries. And it's no later than now!"

"Yes! Yes! It's time...," some commanders were yelling as a sign of support for Perry.

John arrives in Russia from a plane that he boarded in Europe, more precisely in England. The delegation is formed of only one American advisor and several people from some other NATO and the Warsaw Pact countries. Vatievski and his team are already there waiting for them. The Russian leader doesn't look particularly happy because it's a question of war and everybody knows his firm position to don't draw back in front of the American threat. The two leaders and their respective staff enter the room that was arranged for the occasion. It's not a face to face dialogue. Each of the specialists and some UN experienced members is presenting their concerns about the conflictual situation. But the primary goal is to bring Vatievski to sign and accept to cross his arms and dismantle the army. It's now the Russian leader's turn to speak:

"I think that you all want Russia to be weak. Why don't you leave us alone? You don't have to follow us all the time by arranging all kinds of meeting that we obviously don't need."

John raises his finger as he states:

"General Vatievski, I want you to understand the dangerous situation that you contribute to. You are in a panic, and you're pointing guns at people for nothing. And most of all, your strategists already warn that you can't win the west."

"The strategists don't know the battlefield... They live in offices and nice houses. They don't know the strength of Russia. Bring your armies in, and we'll show you..."

"That's exactly what we want to avoid. We don't want to bring any army in... And last, of all, my colleagues and I are ready to offer you one and a half billion dollars to keep Russia as a peaceful country."

"I'm sorry, I must refuse that. I will only accept a conquered west,

controlled by Russia."

"Then you'll regret this in your coffin because you have just made general Perry the happiest man on earth. He will be delighted to burn your entire army and yourself."

All the members of the two delegations are leaving. They're walking thru the alleys of the building. Everybody is talking about the fact that Vatievski is an impossible man. And, there is also the fact that none of the two countries have access to their nuclear arsenal, which is, of course, one less problem to worry about. But deep inside him, John thinks that the world still has two significant obstacles to complete peace: Perry and Vatievski. John is considering to find the reason why Pepper accepted to support Perry. It's like life hasn't changed at all since the day John started to work with Pepper. He never took any decision to order death. If it were the case, he would have immediately kill Vatievski.

Pepper is still the smartest because he knows too well how deceitful the official and legal world can be. Apart from being worst than the underworld. Since the day Perry asked him to be part of the future government, he contacted the WESTSIDE-CONS and put himself on active duty.

They already fix him to eliminate Fanengen. On the other hand, Pepper knows perfectly well that Perry won't make it because the structures of the army will stop him. That's the reason why he got back home with the gang to take cover. It's straightforward, Perry is under the command of the President, and he could slip by arrogating too much power that doesn't belong to him.

For quite a long time, Fanengen had to avoid travelling to go anywhere. But he has to see a friend in France and his group confirmed that they're not able to assure his security. He must always be careful where ever he has to go. The power and the strength of the WESTSIDE-CONS are tremendous. But the old man is brave, and he wants to do everything like in the early days. He will take his helicopter and cross the border from Switzerland to France when he feels like it. Are People always able to evaluate things and see what they can do from what they can't? "Peper" is waiting for Fanengen, not like a kamikaze, but as a professional soldier who will do his job. It's not every day we have a man like that in the streets beyond all the civilians.

He's in Europe on a false identity - a routine to erase every traces that could lead to him thru any enquiry. The man is not rusty at all. Because of John, he had to keep a low profile in the underworld to avoid the internal purge. If he didn't arrange that fictitious resignation from WESTSIDE-CONS, Ann and many people would have caused the gang to fall apart.

Pepper never likes to delegate essential tasks. He did it with John, but it's to be considered a particular case. A man such as Fanengen is a target that only the very best killer should be in charge of that. For now, the champion is still Pepper. The guess would be that it's a little bit out of style for a Prime Minister to take a gun and travel to go assassinate a crime boss. Certainly, Pepper thought it was his duty to send Fanengen where all the completely decayed molecules belong. But the task is enormous. He's not even sure to be able to do it alive, or at least free.

It's 8:30 a.m., Pepper receives a call confirming that Fanengen and his crew will pass by Italy through the Ventimiglia border to go to France. And it will be just before the afternoon. He thinks that a shot of M-72 should be perfect for the occasion. Fanengen's death is part of a big list of people that will enable the gang to erase all traces of their crimes. The last missions to solidified the establishment of the most controversial and troubling kind of business group. Does law offense have a certain logic? From Pepper's standpoint, crime is like doing and taking what you want and destroy the obstacles whether they're humans or not. Around three o'clock p.m., France's La Garde Nationale police corps arrested Pepper after verifying his false identity. The undercover officers stated that the man is Brant Kemp or Wesley Bradford. After talking to the U.S. embassy in Paris that confirmed the incorrect name as being right according to the files of the State Department. While walking thru the corridors, he stops by a speaker saying:

"Mr. Christophe "Lyon" Fanengen was killed this morning when his helicopter was shot down by an anti-tank weapon. The one who was considered as being Europe's top crime boss controlled his criminal empire for more than fifty years. "Lyon" terrorized most of Europe's big cities with frequent gunfights and executions. The authorities always kept their eyes closed on Mr. Fanengen's crime affairs. His numerous political connections made him the untouchable high-rank criminal of the continent. Law enforcement members from Geneva confirmed that the death of Mr. Fanengen will certainly have some violent international repercussions in the underworld. North-American powerful WESTSIDE-CONS group couldn't wish a better time to completely destroy the European gangs originally controlled by Fanengen."

It's like there was no more light nowhere. When John officially contacted Perry to tell him the negotiations failed with Vatievski, he wasn't surprised at all. The President was informed, and Perry ordered the assault by the German border. In Russia, the original invasion plan by Alaska was requested. On the other hand, more stupidity invaded the minds and hearts, and nobody couldn't distinguish anything - the truth or the lies. Since there must always be something to do, either to have a somewhat active, maybe to entertain. John is sure about that. Actually, that's the basis of his success in life. He knows that people don't fight wars or do cruel things while thinking that they shouldn't. It's the self-destruction instinct because what's not good for somebody is not in anyone interest. A human being equals another one.

The wars ignited over the face of the earth like campfires. On his part, John is the world Deliverer who still believes in what he's doing to bring the planet to peace and calm. Things could have been better if somebody was smart enough to order him to "waste" Vatievski. Since killing somebody almost never comes to his mind, he's touring the world for diplomacy. Even though he wasn't able to convince Vatievski, he's still successful.

As the situations are deteriorating to give more work to John, the gang hired some independent killers. Pepper is leading WESTSIDE-CONS activities while waiting for an official position in the US with Perry. The Senator of North-Carolina is an essential target because he wants to break the gang. Strangely, he's now convinced of John's goodwill, and he trusts him. Some people make great revelations before their death. There is no exception for a powerful and prestigious US Senator. Many doctors are trying to stabilize his life at a Navy hospital in Maryland. It's been confirmed that he will not survive.

Of course, nobody dies alone or maybe we should state that a person never almost passed away by himself. The Great "Pepper" crossed the path of Jean "Trigger" Verdio, a very talented gunfighter who can use three to four weapons at the same time. The meeting took place in Atlanta while Pepper was accompanied by "Blaster." An emergency vehicle picked up the two dead bodies because "Blaster" covered for Westley as any bodyguard would have done. According to John, their mistakes were that they took killing for a game - maybe a dangerous game. It's more than that, the activity is a constant dead-end situation. The armed actors of the underworld are people who can't even assume for a minute that a man is able to desire something good for his fellow or directly his neighbor. Although the exterior world had a bad influence on John because of his youth, he came to realise that he's what he admires. And he's in love with the idea that a man can desire good things for his fellows.

Many opponents came to beat Vatievski in Russia and Perry in the US. John felt like there was no surprise because everything is supposed to be in his favor. After all the deaths were buried in wait of some mysterious, magical or godly process to bring them back to life, he installed his super international welfare economics government. Indeed, the most significant success of his career. At the moment, a Chinese man is the British Prime Minister, while a Japanese is the US President. Not only that, John came to figure out a system where nobody is directly submitted to any government. It's too complicated to explain, but it works very well. The catch in John's creations is that they were the standard step in human's life on the planet. He's not better than anybody. Absolutely nothing more than any other man.